MW00891150

Other Books by Ainsley St Claire

If you love Venture Capitalist: Flawless, you might enjoy the other sensual, sexy, and romantic stories and books she has published.

In a Perfect World

Venture Capitalist: Forbidden Love

Venture Capitalist: Promise

Venture Capitalist: Desire

Venture Capitalist: Temptation

Venture Capitalist: Obsession

Venture Capitalist: Longing
(June 2019)

Venture Capitalist*: Enchanted*
(September 2019)

Venture Capitalist: Gifted
(November 2019)

Venture Capitalist: Fascination
(February 2020)

Ainsley St Claire

VENTURE CAPITALIST

Book 6

A Novel

Venture Capitalist: Flawless/Ainsley St Claire—1st edition

About Flawless

A receptionist with a secret. An analyst stretched thin. A billionaire's revelation could tear them apart.

Constance pretends she doesn't have a father. It might as well be the truth with the way the tech mogul denies her existence. So when she falls for her handsome co-worker, she's horrified to learn that her deadbeat dad is his Silicon Valley idol.

Parker grew up with strong family ties. So when his mother suffers through a horrible car accident, he can barely focus his attention on sleuthing out a corporate mole. But with his family and professional life in turmoil, he knows he must somehow find a way to woo the receptionist who's stolen his heart…

After Constance's estranged father announces plans to leave her billions, Parker's fanboy routine makes her worry their pasts are too different for romance to survive.

Can Constance and Parker heal a billion-dollar rift before their passion goes broke?

Flawless is book 6 in the sizzling Venture Capitalist romantic suspense series. If you like white-hot passion, burning mysteries, and smoldering bachelors, then you'll love Ainsley St Claire's scrumptiously steamy novel.

This book is dedicated to Michael and Steven. Two near and dear friends who didn't know each other and passed away long before their time. Without them the Venture Capitalist series would never have existed. I miss you both tremendously.

Prologue

PARKER

One month ago

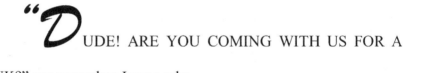

“DUDE! ARE YOU COMING WITH US FOR A DRINK?” my coworker James asks.

It’s been a rough day. I’ve worked for SHN for over a year, and Pineapple Technologies has just gone public. We were their sole investor, and we’ve been celebrating all day as the culmination of our hard work comes together. Now the team wants to gather for drinks after work at The Downstairs Bar. We seem to hang out there often, mostly because it’s close.

“Just give me ten more minutes and I’ll be right there.” As a software analyst at SHN, it’s my job to review other people’s code, test it, and check their math. Currently I have eighteen companies looking for funding from the venture capital firm I work for. Each company would prefer three to five million dollars. I’m the first step in the cog for them to get funding.

Shutting down my computer, I see several of the partners still in the office. They work harder than anyone else here.

A few minutes later I arrive at the bar and see one of the partners, Emerson, sitting with the most beautiful woman I’ve ever seen. She’s breathtaking with her long blonde hair, delicate features, and piercing blue eyes. I can't help but stare. She smiles as she talks and it reaches her eyes.

I'm so busy watching her that I'm not paying attention to where I'm going and almost stumble and fall. Finding my friends from work, I nod my hello. "Who's that woman Emerson's talking to?"

James looks around and spots the two women. "I don't know, man."

"She's hot."

James looks at her again and says, "I suppose, if you're into that kind of girl."

"What kind of girl are you into?"

"Well, last night was a twofer."

"You banged two girls in one night?" My voice pitched high in disbelief. I know San Francisco has more straight females than straight men, but I've yet to meet a real woman who will just sleep with a guy because he's there and has a pulse. I know they must exist somewhere, but the fact that he got two women to sleep with him—he's a chubby guy with greasy hair—I find it difficult to believe.

"This town's screaming full of single women looking to have itches scratched. I just happen to be the guy willing to do it." James makes it sound much simpler than it really is. Well, unless you pay for it, and it wouldn't surprise me if he did.

I roll my eyes. *What a jerk.*

"Well, I think she's hot."

"You know Emerson. Why don't you just go there and introduce yourself?"

Easier said than done. Aside from the fact that Emerson is one of the partners in my firm and my indirect boss, I would never be so brazen to assume I wouldn't be interrupting anything.

I drink my beer and listen to the guys talk about baseball. They're my coworkers, and I like most of them, but they're not really my friends. James is great to work with, but that's where my adoration for him stops.

Only half listening to the conversation, I watch as the woman who has enraptured me finishes her talk with Emerson and shakes her hand. I like that she's tall, and aesthetically, she's damn perfect. Her lithe body fills out the suit she's wearing beautifully. I'd love the chance to get to know her better.

chapter ONE

PARKER

I'M LATE FOR WORK. I don't normally oversleep, but I worked all weekend to prepare for a meeting with my manager, Cameron. He's one of our founding partners, and I like working for him. He's probably the smartest guy I've ever met, and he lets me do my thing and gives me as much rope as I need. I haven't hung myself—yet.

There are four companies I've reviewed that I'm going to pass along for others to vet. I'm fairly confident that three of them are sound investments for SHN, though I'm on the fence about the other one. I keep going back and forth on why I'm struggling. I do know that, despite my thinking the technology is something that will work, the proposals will go to several other groups within SHN and can be kicked by any of them. I want to talk to Cameron about it during our meeting so he's up to date on what my thoughts are.

Exiting the elevator, I'm looking at my phone and walk right by reception before I hear, "Excuse me. Excuse me, sir?"

I look up and it's the blonde-haired beauty from the bar last month, the angel who haunts my dreams. I don't know what to say, but she comes running over. "Hi. My name's Constance. Do you work here?"

I nod, still not knowing if I can speak to her or why she's stopping me. Her voice is even better than I ever imagined. She's wearing a tight pink turtleneck sweater that highlights the pink in her delicate cheeks, and she's shorter than I am even in her heels. My cock stirs in my pants.

"May I see your badge?" she asks. "I was instructed that the new policy allows no one to pass without an ID badge."

We've had some issues with some sensitive information being hacked or shared, and I'd heard our security team was recommending we push out some new policies and procedures. Maybe if I had been on time today, I'd know what those policies are.

Her smile reaches her eyes and my stomach turns. She's even more beautiful than I remember. I can't get past her ice blue orbs, lost in their depths. Her lavender shampoo invades my senses and makes me want to reach out and touch her blonde hair. And at that moment when our eyes meet, I'm sure the world stops spinning. Everything else falls away until we are the only two people left on the planet.

My breath catches, a dozen questions I want to ask her flashing through my mind. I want to know where she lives, if she has a boyfriend, or a husband, or—God forbid—kids. I want to know everything, but nothing comes out of my mouth as I stare at her like I'm an idiot.

I finally reach into my pocket and flash her my ID; it's a terrible picture, so I hate to wear it. I try to smile, but it's so forced that I'm sure I look like a jerk. *Great first impression!*

"Thank you. Have a great day," she singsongs as I walk away.

I finally find my voice—sort of. "You too," I mumble.

Have a great day? Perfect, I'm screwed.

chapter TWO

CONSTANCE

I KNOW IT'S ONLY MY THIRD WEEK AT SHN, but I like it here. I enjoy the work, and I like the people. After I finished my bachelor's degree at Harvard, I wasn't sure I wanted to move back to the Bay Area. My mom drives me crazy about my father, and she needs me. He comes and goes in and out of her life, and my aunt and I are the only ones who are there for her.

My undergrad degree is in English. Not exactly one that sets you on a path for a career, but I knew I wanted to work in the venture capital world. I think I inherited my father's entrepreneurial spirit, so watching ideas move from a paper napkin to a full-fledged plan always intrigued and excited me.

Moving from the napkin typically comes from money, or in most cases venture capital. That's where I want to work and learn. Once I got that figured out, I did a lot of research and decided that I only wanted to work at SHN. Since I didn't have a degree in technology or even finance, I knew I needed to start at the bottom, take whatever I could, and work my way up. I waited for the right opening, and when it happened, I applied and thankfully got the job, since I had no backup plan if things fell through. And I love it here.

The main line rings. "Thank you for calling Sullivan Healy Newhouse. How may I direct your call?" SHN's the premier venture capital fund in the Bay Area. It was founded by Mason Sullivan, business guru; Dillon Healy, finance expert; and Cameron

Newhouse, technology wizard. They met in college and started the fund with their own money when they were all twenty-eight years old while working at various start-ups. For the first two years, they invested in early companies as hobbies. SHN became a real company when one of their client's companies sold for more than quadruple their initial investment.

"Constance?"

My stomach drops. It's my mother. "Yes, Mom." She used to work many years ago, and that's how she met my father. After I was born, she worked occasionally, but has really only survived on handouts from my father or the generosity of others. She no longer understands the importance of a good work ethic. She can also be emotionally fragile, so I always tread carefully.

"I talked to your dad today."

I close my eyes and take several deep breaths. My father's the reason my mother's so damaged. "That's nice. I'm at work. Can we talk about this tonight?" *Or maybe never?*

"Well, he just made my day, and I wanted to share it with you. He was so sweet. He came by, and we spent some time together…"

I stop listening. I know what she's going to say. It's been this way my entire life. My father arrives in her life, and she stops everything for him. She gets so excited for the attention he pays her and promises he makes that he never keeps, and then she's wrecked. He's been married to another woman for years, yet he still comes over and sleeps with my mom regularly.

My parents weren't married when I was conceived, and in all my twenty-five years, my father has had zero interest in being a part of my life. He would make a promise to my mother about spending time with me, we'd spend hours preparing for our "date," and then he'd never show. My first memories are of me wearing a pretty pink dress, having spent what seemed like hours getting ready, and the disappointment of his not showing. When she'd call him, he'd make a lame excuse and she'd forgive him, but after it happening time and again, I've chosen to never forgive him.

I learned a long time ago that what he promises my mother is worthless. It was probably just to feed her what she wanted to hear so he could get on with the part of his life that doesn't include her without any negative publicity.

The only time my mom did have clarity regarding him was when he told her he was going to marry Lauren. She figured out he'd been lying to her for years. I think he promised her they would get married one day when he tired of his bachelor ways and his company was doing well. I was seven when he announced his engagement to Lauren; Mom and I moved to Hawaii for two years. By then he had founded and ran one of the Bay Area's largest companies and is now recognized as the pioneer of the microcomputer revolution, but he still came around sometimes. I could always tell, since my mom was happy and fun to live with around those visits. Then he'd ignore her for a few days, and she'd fall into a depression.

He's an ass as far as I'm concerned. Fuck him and how he treats us. I know it sounds heartless, but my mother could've told him years ago to pound sand and she didn't, so she's made her own bed, and now she can sleep in it.

"… so I thought you might do that."

"Wait, what? What am I doing?" She's always rambling, and then the next thing I know, I'm going on a date with some guy she met randomly or sitting with some yogi she thinks will solve all of our problems.

"Meeting your dad for lunch tomorrow. He works close by you and wants to see you."

"Mom, we've talked about this a thousand and ten times. He has no interest in me. He was only a sperm donor. I know he loves you, but he denies I'm his daughter despite paternity tests. He'll never show up."

"Never say never," she singsongs.

"Mom, the other line's ringing and I need to answer it. Have a good day, and I'll try to call tonight." The other line isn't ringing, but I don't want to get into this personal conversation while I'm at work.

"Okay, honey. Have a good day, and call me when you get home."

I hang up and just sit there. My mother let that man treat her poorly her entire adult life. I decided when I was thirteen that I'd never do that to myself. She takes anything bad I say about my dad personally. He's a narcissist and self-serving. He doesn't want to make time for me, so I don't make time for him.

When I look up, I see Parker getting off the elevator. My heart beats triple time as I look into his earnest, gorgeous hazel eyes.

The flecks of gold in his eye color seemed richer and brighter than usual. Parker Carlyle's easily the hottest guy I've ever seen, and I can't tear my gaze away from his face.

"Good morning, Parker." My stomach clenches and my insides do a somersault, he's so handsome. Unfortunately, he seems to know it. He never looks at me. I'm still embarrassed about my first day when I didn't allow him to pass without a badge. I was only doing what I was told, but he's never seemed to forgive me.

"Hey" is all he says in return as he rushes by me with his eyes averted, the earbuds in his ears slightly humming from the music playing in them.

Behind him, Greer walks in. She's so sophisticated and just seems to have it all together. Greer's one of the partners, and she's our public relations goddess. She's helped to make some of the most complex start-up applications understandable to people on Wall Street, and she's absolutely instrumental to our success.

"Good morning, Greer."

"I brought you a treat. Here's a peppermint mocha." She places the venti white cup on my desk with her name on the side, and I can smell the peppermint. I've already had one this morning, but between my mother's call and Parker being curt with me, I'm due a treat.

"This is my favorite. Thank you."

"I pay attention, and you take such good care of me when I work remotely from Napa." She telecommutes from a winery since her delicious Italian fiancé owns a vineyard. When I grow up, I want to be her.

"I still need to get up to your fiancé's tasting room."

"You're welcome anytime. I promise a behind-the-scenes tour if you do come up."

I'll seriously be considering that. I just love her.

She waves as she leaves, and I take a deep whiff of the peppermint, chocolate, whipped cream, and coffee. Whoever invented this was a pure genius. It's my drug of choice, and I love it.

Dillon and Emerson arrive next. Emerson's my boss, and she runs all things operational around here and with our clients. She also has it all together, and with a handsome husband to boot. She's so accomplished in her own right, having sold her company to SHN and becoming a partner. The story is that Dillon saw her speak at a technology conference about the importance of a team, and he wanted her and her company.

I'll never understand how they can work together and stay married. They don't fight at work, but I've seen her throw the evil eye at Dillon before. I have no doubt that he's not easy to live with.

"Hi, Constance," she greets me. "How's your day going so far?"

"Not too bad. Pancakes and sausage are set up in the break room, and the big coffeepot is full. The phones are just beginning to pick up. I have a list of things that we're running low on in the kitchen, and I've gone through the supply closet and added a few things we need to replace."

Dillon nods in approval. Eyeing my coffee cup, he says, "You better watch out, Emerson. I see Greer's plying her with coffee from downstairs. She's going to snag Constance away from you."

Emerson winks at me. "She better not, but if she were to steal Constance away, it would be an amazing opportunity for her, I'm sure." Dillon gives Emerson a peck on the cheek. It's so nice to feel appreciated. "Let's meet later this morning and go over your list, Constance. I have a few things to add. You're really on it. We'll need to find you more work, so you don't get bored."

"I'd love that. Just let me know." Ordering meals and supplies will quickly become a little mind-numbing, so I'm open to whatever they want to throw at me.

The next thing I know, it's after eleven. Needing to wrap up what's left of breakfast and prepare for the lunch catering to arrive, I walk into the break room. Cameron's there with Parker, having what looks like a very serious conversation. They stop and look at me when I enter.

"Oh, excuse me. I'll come back later." I turn and essentially run away.

I hear Cameron say, "Please, feel free to stick around. Don't let us keep you from your job. All the conference rooms are busy, and we're going through a few proposals. Nothing super-secret." He flashes me a smile, and if I weren't partially frightened of him, I'd probably have a work crush on Cameron. I've met his fiancée though, and not only is she gorgeous, but she's a very accomplished pediatrician here in San Francisco who works in underserved areas.

"Thank you. I won't be long."

Then I see the mess these guys made this morning getting their breakfast. None of the women I know have breakfast in the office very often—unless it's the breakfast burritos. Those, I've discovered, are loved by everyone. But this morning it's like they spilled maple syrup everywhere. Yuck!

There isn't much to pack up, so I put some elbow grease into the sticky mess on the countertops and pull the appropriate hotplates for our Indian feast coming shortly. Just as I finish, I hear the main phone line ringing, so I toss the sponge back into the sink and go answer the phone.

When lunch arrives, I take the food into the break room and get it set up. We have about two dozen restaurants we order from each month, and I'll occasionally find something unique. We have a few vegetarians, some who eat gluten-free, others who are lactose intolerant, and a vegan, so it gets difficult if I need to accommodate everyone. Our firm supplies breakfast and lunch most days, and if we're in crunch time—which is about two weeks of the month—we have dinner catered in. It gets a little boring having the same meals, so I'm always on the lookout for new places that will cater. Last month I found a Basque restaurant that catered a great lunch of lamb, several bean side dishes for my vegetarians and vegans, and potatoes. We eat well every day.

As I set everything up for lunch, Parker wanders over and turns up his nose. "What's for lunch today?"

I turn and smile at him. "Indian."

"Why didn't anyone tell me? Yuck!"

"Well, it's e-mailed to you at the beginning of the month in the company newsletter." I write the newsletter, so I'm trying not to be bothered that he's ignored it. "And it's posted on the refrigerator. I'm happy to put it somewhere else where you might see it. A stall in the men's restroom, perhaps?"

He just glares daggers at me and then stalks away.

All right then.

Watching his back as he leaves, I decide I'm giving up on this guy. He may make my panties wet, but he's a typical twentysomething male in San Francisco and thinks he's God's gift to the world.

chapter

THREE

PARKER

I ACTUALLY LIKE INDIAN FOOD, so I don't know why I made such a stink. I'm an asshole. I just don't know how to act around her. I'm usually pretty good at the flirting thing, but for some reason with Constance, I'm a jerk.

I'm going to just bury myself in my work and try to forget about it. I seem to be on a celibacy kick, not wanting to deal with the hassle just to get laid. I think I'd like a real relationship—but one that's drama free. I haven't found that since moving here to San Francisco, or maybe ever.

My job here at SHN's to work with Cameron, our technology partner. I've seen some amazingly cool shit. I've seen technology that seems silly—3D video conferencing is one—but has so many other applications that are mind-blowing. And I've seen redesigns of search engines that aren't as powerful as the current technology.

Working at SHN's a dream job for me. I heard Cameron speak at a conference in Chicago for one of my classes at the University of Illinois at Urbana-Champaign. He was a speaker at a forum on complex data solutions. I was just a freshman at the time, but all of a sudden, I knew what I wanted to do for a career.

I live and breathe SHN. I know my findings can determine if we're going to invest a lot of money into some of these start-ups. They're all good ideas, but often the technology isn't there to make them realities. Sometimes it can take doing complex math to figure out the design, and other times it takes looking over their business plan and the code. I love what I do, but I also know that not many people can do this.

An instant message shows up on my computer: **Parker, can you join us in Mason's office?**

One of our biggest public offerings, Pineapple Technologies, went sideways the night they went public because someone hacked their highly encrypted system and shared their private information on the web. We got out by selling enough to cover our investment, but it would've made our bonus a banner year. I originally approved the technology as one of the first companies I reviewed as an intern. It's believed the hack was an "inside job," and I know all the partners have been behind doors dealing with the fallout.

I grab my moleskin notebook and a pen and walk to Mason's office. Inside are the three founding partners, but also three people I'm not familiar with.

"Thanks for coming in," Mason greets me.

I nod and take an empty seat in the back.

"Parker, these are Agents Baron and Perry with the FBI." They nod and I return the gesture. "And this is Jim Adelson with our security team."

I've seen Agent Baron around. I wouldn't want to meet him in a dark alley at night. He's kind of scary looking. Agent Perry's female. I don't know why it surprises me that she would be in the FBI. She's very pretty with short, curly, blonde hair and blue eyes.

"Nice to meet you," I mumble.

Cameron turns to me. "Parker, you know about the debacle with Pineapple Technologies." I nod and he continues. "You worked on them initially and know their software code better than their own designers. You and I are going to be part of an FBI task force to ferret out the reason someone was able to hit their 256-bit encryption and get access to all their sensitive data."

"Whatever I can do to help." This is totally awesome. I'm a total geek, and digging in this deep will be a great challenge. And to do it alongside the FBI and security experts is a dream I never had but has come true.

"Great. You both can go through all the code line by line, see if there are any holes and how it may have gotten there," Agent Perry explains.

"What's our timeline?" I ask.

Agent Baron takes over. "We want your thorough review as quickly as you can."

"We can do some cursory work and then give you a timeline. That kind of encryption's extremely complex." Turning to me, Cameron asks, "How many lines of code do you think their technology ran on?"

"One hundred thousand, maybe two hundred and fifty thousand lines. It's been a while since I looked at it, but it took me my twelve-week internship to review and report on. I was young, but it was pretty complex."

The conversation becomes really convoluted at that point, and I just sit back as the security expert explains things to the two FBI agents.

"Our team in cybercrimes will appreciate the help, and we can put them in touch with you," Agent Perry shares.

We end the meeting, agreeing to have our initial meeting to touch base in a week.

When I return to my desk, I can smell the Indian food. Masala, curry and turmeric all work together to make outstanding blends of great food. I load up a plate and include several pieces of naan, then stop by Constance's desk. "I'm sorry about earlier. I thought the smell was burnt rubber. I love Indian food, and you made my day by ordering lamb masala—it's my favorite. Thank you."

"I'm glad you like it. Lamb masala's my favorite, too. There's a great place in Oakland if you ever need the best place for Indian food in the entire Bay Area."

"Thanks. I'll let you know."

When I leave her desk, I can't help but wonder if she was asking me out.

chapter

FOUR

CONSTANCE

I WALK INTO THE SALAD RESTAURANT close to our office and see my best friend studying her cell phone while waiting for me. I've been so busy since starting at SHN that I haven't had time to see her lately, and I've missed her.

Tonya's known me since we started middle school together. She had just moved from China, and girls were cruel to her because of her accent. Most of my classmates thought I was a scholarship kid—my dad paid for school, but he never paid for anything else, so I essentially *was* a scholarship kid, just not a school scholarship—so in their view I was a second-class citizen at a prestigious all-girls school. Tonya and I bonded over boys and a love of the band NSYNC. Together we managed the mean girls and created a great support system, and our parents allowed us to spend tons of time together.

Eventually we chose the same competitive high school, where she graduated as valedictorian and I was third in our class. It was hard work for both of us, and we spent lots of time dreaming about boys and our perfect futures. After graduation, she went to MIT and I went to Harvard, and since both are in Cambridge, Massachusetts, we were roommates all through college.

Her father moved to the Bay Area and founded a robotics company that she now works for, running the research and development group for them. She's very boy crazy even today, but her dad keeps her on a tight leash, and she still lives at home.

"Connie!" She's one of the few who are allowed to call me by my nickname. I stopped letting people call me that when I was fifteen and the mean girls said it was a white-trash name. It broke my mom's heart that they were so mean, but she embraced Tonya as a second daughter and my savior.

Tonya pulls me into a tight hug.

"I know it's only been three weeks, but I sure have missed you."

"I've missed you, too. I have my dad almost convinced to let me live with you in our apartment." She pays half the rent on our apartment in the Marina neighborhood but doesn't live there. I feel super spoiled having a two-bedroom apartment to myself.

"Tonya, that'd be awesome. You could finally move into your bedroom."

"Shh." She looks around cautiously. "My dad has spies everywhere." Breaking out in a case of the giggles, she links arms with me and we get in line to order our salads. "How are you liking SHN? Any cute boys?"

"I love my job. I started at the bottom, but I know this was my chance to get in, and I'll work hard to prove myself. How are things going with your dad?"

"He keeps introducing me to all these Chinese men. Gross. *So* not my type. They smell like fish—yuck! You know I like them blond-haired and blue-eyed."

"If you keep talking like that, your dad will never let you move out."

"Oh, I know it. I often wish he were as distant as your dad."

"Our fathers are the extremes. How about we find a dad somewhere in the middle? Oh, speaking of the sperm donor, my mom saw him a few days ago and she's trying to set up lunch between us."

Tonya scoffs. "When will she learn?"

"I stopped asking after she carted me twenty-five hundred miles away to Hawaii and he still came around."

"I know. We need to find you a nice guy who'll treat you like the crown jewel we all know you are."

"I think we all deserve that."

• • •

We order our salads and find seats in the corner, then gossip our lunch hour away. It goes by in a flash.

I check the time on my phone and tell her, "I need to get back up to SHN."

"Okay. Hey, I'm going to stay in the apartment this weekend. I thought we'd go out and scout out some cute boys."

"You're welcome to stay whenever you'd like. You pay half the rent, after all. I'll think about going out. This job has me exhausted at the end of each day, and you know me, I'd rather stay home and read a book instead of getting all dressed up to have some guys drool all over me for a one-night stand."

"Oh we're going out. I'll be there on Friday night by seven."

We embrace and wave goodbye.

"See you then," I call over my shoulder as I walk away. "I'll be the one in my pajamas with my Kindle in hand."

When I return to the office, Emerson's sitting at reception. I look at my phone and note that I'm not late—I don't think.

She sees me and smiles. "You're back already?"

"I'm sorry I took too long. I thought Bernie was covering for me. I didn't mean to inconvenience you."

"You didn't, not at all. I sent Bernie to lunch and took over. It's a good reminder of how the office works. But your lunch hour *is* an hour, and you haven't left for lunch since you started. We aren't slave drivers here. If your lunch occasionally lasts longer than an hour, we're okay with that."

She stands to leave and hands me a pink message slip. "You got a message from your dad's office trying to schedule lunch with you and him. I took down her number since she wasn't sure if you had it."

I take the paper and crumple it as I put it in my pocket. "Thanks," I mumble.

"Take the time you need if you want to meet him for a long lunch."

"Oh, that's very kind of you, but I'll meet him over the weekend. He always wants to try to meet during the week, but he always has something come up and cancels."

"Whatever you need." She smiles. "Go to the bathroom and grab a drink before you get going again. It'll be a busy afternoon."

I do as she suggests, and when I return to my desk, I call my dad's office. I have the number, but I only call if it's an absolute must.

Ruthie has been my dad's secretary since before I was born. She was there while my parents bickered over paternity and throughout their thirty-year affair; she knows where all the bodies are buried.

She doesn't answer, so I leave a message. "Ruthie, it's Constance. Please thank my dad for the lunch invitation, but I've recently started a new job, and I'm not able to take time off. Another time maybe."

That's as polite as I can be under these circumstances. I'm sure she understands.

chapter

FIVE

PARKER

I TEXT CAMERON AS A REMINDER. **I have that meeting with the FBI cyber team this morning. I'm not sure how long it'll take. I have the files for Symcode, Accurate, and The Kindness Project on my desk if anyone needs anything.**

Cameron: Thanks. Priority one is Pineapple.

Me: Understood. I'll let you know what I learn when I return.

Walking into the FBI building is quite different than you'd see on TV. For one, it's nondescript. Located in the financial district, it seems to hide between giant financial buildings, but at the same time it sticks out. There's no awning over the front door, nothing but concrete all around the building. No potted plants or greenery of any kind, and the people entering are not in thousand-dollar suits. I can't figure out what else makes it peculiar until I notice the windows all have closed blinds compared to the open ones like all the other buildings around it.

Walking in, I'm not greeted. The woman behind the desk sits with two obviously armed guards standing on each side of her; both look like linebackers who'd seem more comfortable on a football field than security. Nothing in her scowl says "Welcome"—rather she looks bored as she watches me cross the foyer, waiting for me to tell her why I'm here. I must be interrupting the important game of solitaire she's playing on her computer or whatever it is she's doing.

"Hi. My name's Parker Carlyle, and I'm here to meet with Agent Cora Perry in Cybercrimes."

"Your ID please."

I place my driver's license in her waiting hand. She carefully looks at the picture and then at me, repeating the action several times. I start to grow concerned. I had that picture taken on my birthday two years ago, and I was pretty hungover. I know my hair's a bit shorter, but I don't think I've changed that much.

"This is a Washington state driver's license. Did you fly down for this meeting?"

"Um… no. I live here in The City. That's my permanent address. I only moved here a few months ago." Okay, it was over a year ago, but who's splitting hairs?

She picks up the phone and tells whoever answers, "I have Mr. Carlyle here, and he doesn't have a valid photo ID. It has an address in Washington state."

She listens a few moments, and I'm sure she's going to refuse me entry. She clicks a few buttons on the computer, then says, "Yes, that address is registered to a Phillip and Marjorie Carlyle."

Those are my parents. How does she know that?

Silence reigns as she listens to the person on the other end of the phone. She isn't making eye contact, and all I can think is how I'm going to explain this to Cameron.

"Okay, I'll let him know." She hangs up the phone and looks at me. "Mr. Carlyle, we typically don't allow people to enter the building with photo IDs that don't match their information, but Agent Perry says you're integral to her investigation. You need to get a local ID and soon." She hands me back my driver's license, and I place it in my wallet.

"Yes, ma'am."

She points me to a security station that's similar to an airport. After passing through the X-ray machines and metal detectors, I'm given a badge, and a man who looks my age escorts me to the eighth floor.

I walk into a room that looks like the engine room on the Starship *Enterprise* and stop short. "Holy cow!"

My escort turns to me with a big grin. "Welcome to Cybercrimes."

I'm stunned by the technology surrounding me. Floor-to-ceiling walls of supercomputers, chairs that look like they belong in jet cockpits, and the people inside are dressed like a bunch of high school dropouts, clustered into groups at desks with multiple monitors. It's like I've died and gone to geek Heaven.

He lets me take it all in for a few moments and then nudges me. "This way, Parker."

He leads me to a room with glass walls, where a small group of people is sitting around a conference table dressed like they haven't slept in a week.

Agent Perry greets me. "Welcome, Mr. Carlyle. Please have a seat." She motions to an empty seat and introduces me to the four other people at the table.

We walk through what I know about what happened with Pineapple Technologies and what I've discovered so far, which isn't much. Agent Perry begins writing on a whiteboard, and slowly but surely, a timeline begins to appear. On one side of the board are four pictures of who they tell me are Russian oligarchs living here in the Bay Area. "We believe these men are behind what's going on," Agent Perry explains. "Our plan's to connect what happened at Pineapple with this group."

Two hours later, I'm in a rideshare back to the office. Part of me is giddy thinking about all the fun this is going to be, but another part of me is bothered by it. How did this happen, and how did SHN get in the middle of it?

Arriving at the office, I walk in and see Constance. She's wearing a light blue sweater and a dark gray pencil skirt. She's beautiful. I nod at her, and she greets me with a small smile.

Heading to my desk, I check my e-mail and voice mail messages, making sure there are no emergencies before I talk to Cameron. All clear.

I knock on the doorframe before entering. He motions for me to come in and I close the door behind me.

"How'd it go?" he asks.

"I should start by assuring you that I love my job here."

He looks at me, obviously waiting for the ball to drop.

"Holy shit, Cameron. I went to the cybercrimes floor, and it puts all the science fiction movies you've ever seen to shame."

Cameron sits back and relaxes. "I could totally geek out there."

"Trust me, I did. The group's chasing some bad players, and they've got some serious tools." I walk him through everything I saw, then the task force and our responsibilities.

"That's great. It looks like you'll need some admin help. Emerson believes Constance will be able to support you."

My stomach drops. How will I ever be able to work with her and not have a raging hard-on? Reining my thoughts in, I clear my throat and say, "Okay, that works. I'll check to see if she has the time to help." I stand to leave. "Thanks. I'll let you know how far I get this afternoon."

I head back to my desk and look over at Constance. She's talking to John, one of the finance guys, and laughing at something he just said. It makes my blood boil.

I walk up, and he eyes me up and down. I look at Constance. "I have a big project I'm working on, and I was told you could help me with Excel and some pivot tables?" Turning to John, I ask, "Did you need something?"

"Nope. Just talking to the beautiful girl in the front." He smiles and winks at her.

"I have work with her to get done. You should leave."

He holds his hands up in mock surrender. "Whatever, man."

Constance looks at me in complete shock. "Was that really necessary?"

"We're here to work, not make dates."

Tears begin to pool at the edges of her eyes. Crap. That was directed at him, not at her. "I meant John needs to be working. You're doing a great job. It's not you. Promise."

"I get that you don't like me very much, but my job's to be nice to everyone, and that's all I'm doing."

"What do you mean, I don't like you very much? I like you a lot. I just need your help, and he's only interested in getting into your pants."

The tears immediately evaporate, replaced by fire as she stands and rests her palms flat on her desk. "Parker Carlyle, you're not his manager, and you're not mine. I'll happily help you with your project, but you don't need to worry about my personal life."

I'm taken aback, and a few people who sit close are watching us, clearly having heard her outburst. "Okay then. I'll have the first round of numbers for you in the morning. Does that work?"

My reaction to Constance is visceral, primal, and I have no damn idea why I feel the need to jump into the mix and make sure everyone knows she belongs to me. Of course, *she* doesn't even know she belongs to me.

Grow a pair, man.

She takes a few deep breaths and seems much calmer now. "Yes, that works. I'm also happy to stay late if you prefer to get going earlier."

"If you're serious about tonight, that would be greatly appreciated. You usually do the ordering in for meals, but since it would just be the two of us, I'm happy to do that. We can meet in the conference room at six if that works for you. I can share our project with you, and then we can brainstorm the best way to manage it."

"I can order dinner. That isn't a problem. What would you like? Mexican? Sushi? Italian? Pizza? Chinese? You tell me."

"Mexican sounds great. How about street tacos from Jose's?"

"That's what I was thinking. See you at six."

That went sideways too fast. I don't know what it is about her that makes me turn all protective. I'm sure she has a father who does that enough.

What was I thinking?

I return to my desk, and through the company instant messaging feature, I fill Cameron and Emerson in on what we've decided. **Constance agreed to help me with the FBI task force. We're going to get a start on it tonight. We're ordering dinner. I'm happy to pay for it if that's a problem.**

Cameron: I may join you. I'll get with Constance.

Emerson: No problem. Do you need other help? Can I do anything?

Me: No, I think we'll get this started. Thank you for suggesting her help. It'll really make a difference.

The office is still buzzing when Constance stops by my cubicle. "Dinner has arrived."

I look at my clock. I've been so immersed in my project that I've lost track of time; the afternoon has already flown by.

As she heads over to Cameron's office to let him know, I bring my laptop to the conference room. Constance's is already there, and Cameron arrives with his computer in his arms moments later. He goes over our project once we're all settled, and she takes notes and asks great questions. When he feels like we're all up to speed on everything, Cameron leaves us to get started, and Constance and I work until after 9:30 p.m. when I see her yawn.

"I'm sorry, I'm keeping you. This project will go on for weeks. I think I'm good for now. I'll continue to work on this and feed you packets of information as I have it."

"I can keep going if you need me."

"No, let's get you a ride home. We can continue tomorrow."

"Okay. Let me get my things and I'll call up a ride."

"What part of town do you live in?" I ask.

"The Marina. How about you?"

"The same. Do you want to share a ride?"

"Sure."

We walk downstairs and wait for the car to arrive, climbing into the back seat together. I love the way her perfume smells, so light and feminine. Sitting next her makes me think about how soft her skin would be. It takes all of my self-control to not reach out and touch her.

As we ride over the hill, she asks, "Where are you from originally?"

I chuckle. "No one's ever from here, are they? I'm from the Seattle area. How about you?"

"I'm one of the few from here. I grew up here in The City."

"A San Francisco native? That's rare. What did your parents do?"

"They both worked in technology."

We arrive at her place, and though I would love for the conversation to continue, I know it's time to call it a night. "See you tomorrow?"

"I'll be there at seven."

"Oh, you don't have to be there that early for the project. Nine's more than fine."

She smiles at me. "No, but I need to be there for my regular duties. Who do you think sets breakfast up and makes all the coffee?"

I feel absolutely stupid. Of course she has to be there early. Today was a long day for her—almost fifteen hours. Jeez, I need to keep an eye on that.

"Oh, right. Well, I'll try not to keep you late often."

“Don’t worry about it. I love the work, and I appreciate the opportunity to show that I can do more than set up catering and answer phones.” She waves and then heads into her building.

Her vanilla perfume and her lavender shampoo linger nicely inside the car after she leaves. I take deep breaths, committing it to memory.

Lying in bed, I keep thinking about Constance. I wonder if anyone calls her Connie. She has a kind of understated beauty; perhaps it’s because she’s so disarmingly unaware of her prettiness. Her alabaster skin’s completely flawless. She’s all about simplicity, making things easy, helping those around her to relax and be happy. Maybe that’s why her skin glows, her inner beauty lighting her deep blue eyes and softening her features. When she smiles and laughs, I can’t help but smile along too, even if it was just on the inside.

After spending the evening with her, I realize she made me feel that I’m important, and a better man. Who wouldn’t want that in their life?

chapter

SIX

CONSTANCE

I'M STILL BUZZING FROM THE RUSH of working on the project, and spending time with Parker. Unable to sleep, I text Tonya. **Guess what? I just got home from a long day at work. I got a new project that may move me out of reception, and I'm working with the cutest boy in our office.**

Tonya: Is it that Parker guy you mentioned?

I'm so excited that she's awake. I can't wait for her to move in. **Yes! He went all crazy protective and then wanted to buy me dinner. I made the firm pay, and we worked on our project.**

Tonya: Did you kiss?

I roll my eyes.

Me: No. We were working.

Tonya: Does he smell good?

Me: Oh yes. He wears this great sandalwood cologne. It's not overpowering at all. I could smell it in the rideshare on the way home.

Tonya: Does he have big hands?

Me: Get your mind out of the gutter.

Tonya: Can you tell how big his package is?

Me: Tonya! I didn't look. It's a professional project.

Tonya: Fine. Did you get his digits?

Me: No, I'll see him at work in the morning.

Tonya: How are you going to move from coworkers to naked playmates?

I smile and shake my head.

Me: What did your dad say about staying with me this weekend?

Tonya: He loves you. He's good with it. I want to wear a short skirt and meet some boys.

Me: Who are you going out with?

I'd rather stay home and sleep, particularly if my days are going to be like they were today.

Tonya: You're silly. I'm going to drag you out. You can change your name if you're worried about someone figuring out who your dad is.

Me: No one at work has figured it out, but Parker asked what my parents did. Luckily we pulled up to the apartment right then, so he couldn't push.

Tonya: Well, we're going to meet some hot guys, bring them back to the apartment, tie them up, and take advantage of them.

Me: I'll have to see how this week plays out. If I have 15-hour days every day for the rest of the week, I'll be mush by Friday night.

Tonya: Pace yourself.

Me: I'm going to bed. Have a good night. Can't wait to see you in four days.

Tonya: Love you!

Me: Love you, too.

I do love Tonya. I'm convinced had her dad told her she could date when we were in school or tell her she can only date a non-Chinese man, she wouldn't be quite so intent on doing the exact opposite. Lying in bed, I think of Parker and his tousled dark brown hair, which was thick and lustrous. I want to run my fingers through it—preferably when he's between my legs. His eyes are a mesmerizing deep hazel blue, filled with flecks of golden light that perform ballets when he gets excited about our project. His face is strong and defined, his features molded from rock. He has dark eyebrows, which slope downward in a serious expression. His usual playful smile draws into a hard line across his face when he's unhappy, but his perfect lips are ripe for the kissing. I think about what his strong hands will feel like if he holds mine as he stares deep into my eyes, and I can't help but blush.

I imagine he's with me now, his smile etching its way back onto his face. His body is warm and toned; I believe if he hugged me, it would be comforting to the touch. His voice is deep, with a serious tone. I fall asleep thinking about what it would be like if his lips brushed my ear as he whispered, "I want you."

chapter

SEVEN

CONSTANCE

IT'S BEEN A LONG WEEK. Parker tries to clear me out most evenings by seven, and because of that, I work on the project around my other duties throughout the day. I'm a little behind, but I'll catch up this weekend.

Sitting in the back of the rideshare, I note that the early evening lull has come to the streets of San Francisco, that quiet between the frenetic commuters and the vibrant party seekers. The clubs are still mostly closed, the only visible life being the restaurant patios that teem with diners, chatting and drinking their beverage of choice and relaxing after a busy day.

Somehow Tonya has talked me into going out tonight. She's met a guy through work who she's agreed to meet at a club in the Tenderloin neighborhood. I'm just going as a buffer. If she hits it off with him, I may head out early. I'm beat, and I can hardly keep my eyes open.

"I'm so happy to be here," she says as her long willowy arms capture me in an unexpected hug when I arrive at the apartment.

"I'm thrilled you're here. Are you sure you want to go out tonight? I'd much rather stay in and catch up with you."

"Oh, we're going out. Darren has a friend he's going to bring for you, so you don't feel left out."

I roll my eyes and cringe. "You know I'm not interested in dating anyone. I'm too busy at work."

"Who said anything about dating? I'm talking about getting lucky," she says with a lot of sass.

I ignore her levity.

"Can I take a power nap?" I feel like my knuckles are dragging on the ground. The only thing that sounds appealing is sleeping for a week straight.

"Yep, we're meeting the guys at ten."

I can't help but be a tiny bit disappointed. Spending time with Tonya is rare, and I want to see her alone. I don't want to share her with anyone.

"Ten? Are you trying to kill me?"

"Nope, just help you find your Prince Charming."

"Wake me at ten fifteen," I beg.

"Oh no. You're going to wear that short pink dress we bought in Cabo last year." The dress is formfitting, exposing lots of cleavage and barely covering my ass. It's a dress that says I'm looking to get laid, though I'd most certainly fall asleep during any foreplay and probably destroy some guy's ego forever if I did that.

"You bought that dress for you. I'll only wear it if I can wear leggings underneath," I stress.

"And hide those gorgeous long legs of yours?"

And my tits and my stomach and everything else. We determined the last time that even a thong was obvious. I'm not going to wear it tonight.

I wave over my shoulder as I drag myself toward my bedroom. "Good night."

"I'll wake you by nine thirty," she calls after me.

"You're killing me." I walk into my room, strip down to my underwear and bra, and crawl between the covers.

I feel like I've just laid down when she turns the lights on. "Okay, Princess Constance, time to wakey-wakey."

I sometimes really hate that Tonya's constantly chipper. Someone could crash her car or steal her favorite purse and she'd still be happy as can be. I envy that in her.

"Go away," I mutter, still hoping the darkness can pull me in.

"I need you. This guy Darren's cute, and I'd like to hang out with him. Can you at least come for a little bit and meet his friend? If you want to leave after that, and I feel safe enough, you can head back here."

I throw back the covers and will myself to sit up. “Fine. I’ll get up.”

She’s laid out my clothes—a very short black dress with a little more length than the pink one she threatened earlier and silver high-heeled sandals. “You’re going to owe me for this.”

“I know. I’m good for it. I promise.”

And I do know she’s good for it. In fact, the scales always tip in her favor, with me owing her more than she owes me.

We meet up with Darren and his buddy John. He seems like a nice guy, and despite how boy crazy Tonya is, she’s a little shy. She’s all talk and no action from living a very sheltered life with a highly domineering father.

The guys know someone at the door, and we’re ushered inside and shown to a table without having to wait.

John turns to me. “What can I get you to drink?”

“A glass of white wine, please.”

Darren does the same with Tonya, and the guys disappear.

“Darren seems like a nice guy.” I watch him worm his way up to the bar with John closely behind. He appears to be a little out of his element and a bit awkward, which gives me comfort that he isn’t a player and won’t take Tonya’s beautiful heart out for a drive before crushing it into smithereens.

“He’s in technical sales, but he doesn’t sell to my group. I don’t think he’s put together that I’m the chairman’s daughter.”

Both of us have powerful fathers, and that works as a double-edged sword. Guys either stay far away because Silicon Valley can be small and a simple word to a few people will end a career, or they see us as trust fund babies. “Do you want him to?”

“Definitely not. He’s polite but not differential, so that helps.”

We enjoy our drinks and John asks me to dance. Inside the club, it’s like dancing on the Northern Lights; an array of blues, acid greens, hot pinks, and gold swirls beneath the dry-ice smoke. The music plays over the dance floor as if fused with the hot, sweaty bodies grinding together to the beat.

The vibes flow like a virus, but a good one. There’s love in the air, all hyped up and ready to give us a good time. Darren weaves through the throng of people like a pro, holding tightly to Tonya’s hand. She’s grinning, and he seems really into her. I’m happy for Tonya.

John and I are clearly not into one another, both just doing our job as best friends do. I'm dancing like this is my last night on Earth, but I think that's just the way my mind avoids thinking about the hangover to come. The music moves me like I'm a puppet on strings, my head mashing so hard my brain is in shut down mode. The strobe lights masks so many of my movements, every clap of my hands like it's on pause at different moments. Tomorrow there will be hell to pay, but tonight the alcohol keeps on flowing like it's on an IV drip.

Last call happens, and we head out. Darren asks Tonya if he can see her tomorrow night—well, actually later tonight—and she agrees. She's grinning from ear to ear, and I can tell she's elated.

John shakes my hand and thanks me for dancing the night away with him. I'm neither offended nor embarrassed; there just wasn't any spark at all between the two of us.

Tonya remains calm until we're in our rideshare heading for a breakfast place close to our apartment. Then she's screams so loud, the driver almost crashes.

"So sorry, she's just super excited about meeting a guy," I explain.

"Next time try not to scream like your friend stabbed you," the driver grumbles.

We smile broadly at him and apologize again during the ride to our favorite breakfast place. It's after two, and I'm tired, but waffles, bacon, and good maple syrup will let me sleep. Hopefully the food with lots of water and orange juice will reduce the hangover, too.

As we order, a group of rowdy guys walks in. I don't pay attention or give them a passing glance until I hear a voice that sounds familiar. "… pick the Seahawks over the 49ers anytime."

He sees me at the same time I see him. It's like we're both frozen in time, neither of us sure what to do. Do I go over and talk to him? Do I ignore him? Do I wave?

I compromise and give him a half-wave.

Tonya asks, "Who are you waving at?"

He returns his own awkward half-wave.

"Parker," I say just above a whisper.

In two-tenths of a second, Tonya has turned in her seat and is gaping at the group of guys. "Holy shit! Those are some cute guys."

Parker looks at his friends and says something, then walks over. "Hey, Constance."

"Hello. What brings you here?"

He's nervous. I see him holding his hands in front of himself, and it looks like he's rubbing his thumb on his palm. "The guys and I were out. I didn't have the energy after our crazy week—"

"Why hello there, ladies." One of the guys from his group of friends has come over to investigate who we are. He's looking at Tonya like she's dinner and he hasn't eaten in a month.

She fidgets nervously while I look at Parker expectantly.

"Get lost, Thad," Parker growls. "I work with Constance, and I'm just saying hello."

"Can't I say hello to the ladies, too?"

Turning to me, he says, "I'm sorry. He's drunk. Normally he's a nice guy."

"That's okay. I'll be in the office on Sunday. We can catch up then."

Thad has pulled up a chair and takes an orange slice garnishment off Tonya's plate. He licks it suggestively, and we're all in shock.

Parker grabs him by the arm and pulls him away. "I'm really sorry."

I can't help but smile and blush a bit. "It's okay."

Tonya leans in with a rushed whisper as soon as they're gone. "OMG! *That's* Parker? I can see why you're so smitten."

"We're coworkers, nothing more."

"He's hot for you."

I roll my eyes. She has no idea what she's talking about.

Throughout my breakfast, Tonya regales me with her excitement about Darren. We know that as time goes on, if it becomes serious, we'll have another mountain to climb with her parents, but for now I want her to enjoy this. She deserves it.

As she talks, I glance over at Parker and his friends. He's sitting off from them, and I can see him watching us. It makes my stomach flutter.

Maybe Tonya's right.

Crawling into bed with a full stomach and my blackout curtains drawn, I'm ready for sleep, and it comes quickly.

I wake when the sun finds a crack between the curtains and shines right on my face. Rolling over like I'm a vampire hiding from the sun, I note that it's almost noon. I know if I don't get up, I'll never sleep tonight and I won't be able to make it through tomorrow.

When I sit up in bed, my head's throbbing with a thousand tiny daggers piercing my brain right between the eyes, I feel a bit nauseous, the hangover excruciating and debilitating. I can smell coffee, and I go in search of the nectar I so desperately need.

As I approach the kitchen, I hear Tonya singing. I stop and listen, trying to place the tune. It takes me a minute, but I finally figure it out: Taylor Swift's "Love Story." It makes me smile that she's so excited.

"It should be a crime to be that happy when you wake up," I grumble.

"I've been up for a few hours. You're the one pulling ten hours with the sandman."

I roll my eyes. "When do you see him tonight?"

"We'll meet here at six thirty, and then we're heading out to dinner. When are you meeting Parker?"

"Tomorrow whenever he shows up at the office. I tend to arrive about two hours before he does during the week, but my job duties are to open the office and get everything all set up."

"You're entirely overqualified for that job."

"I know that, but I can do it for a year." I pour myself a big cup of coffee, then stir in sugar and some milk. "Plus they're already giving me high-profile projects, which is super positive."

"I agree. Now you have to help me figure out what to wear tonight."

"Do you know where you're going to dinner?"

"He mentioned The Italian Restaurant on embassy row." She rolls her eyes. "You'd think they could've come up with a better name."

"Oh, you're going to like it there. We've had food catered from them a few times, and it's always been super good with not many leftovers."

"How dressy is it?"

"I think you'd be fine in your floral print sundress with the pink sweater and your cute sparkly sandals."

"You don't think that's too casual?"

"Not at all. I think you'll look perfect."

"So what should I do with this hair of mine?"

We spend the afternoon getting her ready for her date. I hope it goes well. In school, boys didn't pay much attention to either of us. It never bothered me, but as strict as her parents were at home, she felt that she missed out.

The front buzzer rings at exactly 6:30 p.m., and I give her a big hug before she walks out the door to meet Darren.

My headache has subsided, and now I'm hungry. I order a mushroom and pepperoni pizza and sit myself down to watch a few episodes of *Project Runway*. I actually love the downtime. I don't get it often enough, and I need it to recharge. It's exactly what I've needed—the forced downtime, mindless television, and good pizza. I'll be ready to go tomorrow.

It's after 1:00 a.m. when Tonya comes home, giddy with excitement. We talk for over an hour, and she shares how great the date went and their plans for next weekend.

"I'll be heading into the office about eight. I'm not sure how long I'll be." I give her a big hug. "Text me tomorrow when you head home to your parents' place. And I want to know immediately if you talk to Darren this week." I wag my fingers at her and then blow her a kiss.

"I promise. Good night."

I take a rideshare across town to the office and am shocked that Mason and Dillon are already there working on something. I let them know I'm around, then make a Nespresso instead of a whole pot of coffee and sit in the conference room to start catching up before Parker arrives.

People begin to trickle in over the next hour or so. We have a company going public this week, and it's crazy busy. Mason flies out tomorrow to be at the New York Stock Exchange to ring the bell and do what he calls "pressing the flesh" with several of the banks on Wall Street. Greer told me that we're developing such a strong track record, the big banks are courting us to handle our clients.

When Parker arrives after ten, he asks, "What time did you get here?"

"Not too long ago. I needed to get caught up."

"It was great to see you the other morning at the diner."

"I bet your friend Thad was hurting yesterday morning."

"I think you're right. He never gets like that, but he just got a huge promotion. We went to business school together."

"Where did you go?"

"Chicago."

"Did you always want to work in finance?"

He tells me the story about meeting Cameron and how this is his dream job.

"I'll admit, I'm not in my dream job, but I love it here," I share.

"What's your dream job?"

"SHN's my dream company, don't get me wrong, but jobwise, probably working for Emerson's team. I have a lot to learn. Greer thinks I should work for her team. I think I'd be lucky with either."

Cameron sticks his head in close to lunch and asks for an update. Parker walks him through what he's found and I show him the pivot tables. He seems happy with our progress so far.

"How far do you think you'll be for the next meeting with FBI Cybersecurity?"

Parker looks at me carefully and says, "We can be halfway if I can get some help to cover Constance up front."

Wait! I get to attend the meeting? That's amazing.

Cameron shrugs. "I'll clear it with Emerson and get us a temp." He turns to me and asks, "Could you let the temp in tomorrow morning and prep them for the day?"

"Of course," I assure him.

chapter

EIGHT

CONSTANCE

I'M ENJOYING THE PROJECT IMMENSELY. For now, there's been a temp covering the front desk while we work through this project. I know I'll be going back to the front desk eventually, but working with Parker each day has been fun.

We do the same thing every single day—we work all day, we flirt a little but remain businesslike, and we share a rideshare home to our neighborhood. After two weeks of being together more than eight hours a day, he's still very restrained and all business.

He leans forward, resting his forearms on the table, his hand so close to mine that if he moves just a fraction of an inch, we'll be touching. But I don't need to touch him to feel the sizzle emanating from our attraction. That same sizzle must be rolling off me in waves.

He stands, looking down at me as his body looms close to mine, and I drink in the heat that's coming off him, even from where he stands. His face is angled down at me, and for a split second, I'm certain he's going to kiss me. I lick my lips in anticipation and start to close my eyes when his hand angles my chin away from his face. "You want to go grab a bite to eat, and we can come back to this tomorrow?"

I remember meeting Parker, instantly noticing his handsome features, piercing hazel eyes, shaggy brown hair, and lean body. I also remember trying to stop him from entering because he didn't have a badge, and I'll forever be disappointed that he can't seem to get over that. "Sure, why not? All I have at home is boxed macaroni and cheese and a frozen meal."

We're grabbing dinner on our way home. It's not a date, of course, just coworkers getting together.

We walk into the Greek restaurant in our neighborhood, and my stomach growls in anticipation. I've never been here, but I've always heard great things about it. Light, soothing instrumental music plays over speakers as we're seated at a small table, the candle atop it lighting up his face. I would swear the candlelight makes the golden flecks in his eyes dance. When our knees brush, an electric jolt sends a message to my sex, and I start to wonder if going out to dinner was a mistake.

My stomach rumbles, but there's no way I can eat, not with the knot of anxiety swirling in my gut as I sit so close to him.

The hostess asks, "Would you like something to drink?"

I'm ready to tell her I'm okay with San Francisco's finest drinking water, but Parker turns to me and asks, "Would you like some wine?"

I nod and he turns to the hostess. "We'll take a bottle of the house Restina wine."

"I'll get that for you right now." She turns on her heel and disappears.

"Come here often?" I flirt.

"My sister and I come here when she's in town. We love the house Restina. It's supposed to be made by the owner. We don't have to finish the whole bottle. I just thought it sounded manly to order one."

His admission starts a giggle fit. "Manly?"

"Sophisticated? I'm a little nervous being here with you."

I shake my head and smile, my heart singing with his admission. "I've heard great things about this place. Is there anything you recommend?"

"I haven't had anything I don't like here, but I prefer the souvlaki and the spanakopita. Of course, the pitas are to die for as well."

"Have you had the pastitsio?"

"No, but that's my sister Elizabeth's favorite."

Great, that settles it. I close my menu just as our waiter comes over. In a thick Greek accent, he shares his name and the specials as he pours our wine.

We place our orders, and after the waiter walks away, Parker picks up his glass. "To the beautiful woman who agreed to have dinner with me tonight."

I blush from my head to my toes. And at that moment when our eyes meet, I'm sure the world stops spinning. Everything else falls away until we're the only two people left on the planet. My heart pounds hard, the blood in my veins turning to a roar in my ears. I reach for him, drinking him in like a desert traveler guzzles water in the middle of an oasis. "Thank you for finally asking."

"I hope this means we can see where this takes us?"

I nod. "I'd like that very much." I need to change the subject or I might jump his bones here at the table. "Tell me about your sister."

He smiles. "We're twins, but not identical."

"Well, that's good, or I'd have to say she got robbed in the name department. Either that or you have some explaining to do."

He laughs hard, and I love the sound. I want to capture it and make it my ring tone. "You'd be surprised at how many people ask if we're identical."

"You must be exaggerating."

Our conversation moves to stories of people who ask some of the oddest questions until our dinner arrives. I'm hungry, but I'm not sure my nerves will keep it down. I take my first bite, and it's outstanding and delicious. The perfect blend of ground meat, bechamel sauce, cheese, and pasta.

"If you keep moaning, I may have to leave and take care of myself."

My eyes widen at the comment. He's always been so formal with me, but his attraction makes me feel beautiful—something I rarely feel. "I'm sorry. This is so good."

"Don't be sorry. I love it. This must be better than boxed mac and cheese."

"I don't know. I also have a hot dog. I could've added it to really spice my boxed dinner up."

"How old are you? Isn't that what you ate when you were a kid?"

"No way. My mom's a hardcore vegetarian. It was mac and cheese with tofu. And never from a box."

He grabs his stomach and scrunches up his face. "That sounds terrible." We giggle a bit. "I think the worst thing my mom did was she got really into beets when I was in elementary school, and she would send my sister and me to school with beet salad and goat cheese. I still don't eat beets."

"Beets aren't my thing either. What do you like to eat?"

He looks deep in my eyes and growls, "I eat everything." The innuendo obvious, a moan escapes before I realize it. My nerves ball up in my stomach all over again, reminding me how I react to his touch. My nerves are wound too tight to finish my dinner, and we pack it up before we leave.

"I guess we need to get you home," he says.

He walks me the three blocks to my apartment. Before parting ways, he wraps a hand around my waist and pulls me in for a deep, slow, wet kiss. When we move away, my breath quickens, and I can't find my words for a moment. He whispers something inaudible in my ear, and the feeling of his warm breath on my neck sends chills down my spine.

I don't want this moment to end.

His hands wander along my sides and back, pulling me toward him once more. His tongue takes its sweet time rolling against mine, sending jolts to my core. When we break that time, he says, "I'm sorry. I didn't mean to do that."

I wipe the corners of my mouth and reach for his arm to keep steady. "It was nice," I murmur.

"It was better than nice." He nuzzles my neck, and I'm delirious.

He doesn't move beyond our fantastic kiss. I'm sure he's holding back because of our work relationship. "We can wait until the project is over."

He nods. "Wait? No. I don't want to wait."

"You don't?"

"Definitely not. Let's have a real date tomorrow night. It's Friday, so we can go out for dinner and maybe see a movie. Does that sound okay?"

I nod and smile. "I like that idea—at least the dinner part."

He leans in and kisses me again, invading my mouth with his tongue. The electric charge is back. I'm dizzy with excitement, and I can feel his hard cock pressing at my sweet spot.

Looking to the heavens, he groans, "I've got to go or I won't be going."

I'm so conflicted. I want him to stay. I want to see him naked, I want to taste him. "I know. I feel the same way," I whisper, placing my head on his chest.

I wave goodbye as I enter my building and float upstairs to my apartment.

I can't help but think about how our attraction's actually mutual. My heart flutters at the thought of how tomorrow night will play out. I know working in the same room with him all day will have me wanting to pick up where we left off. It'll be hard, but I have a feeling it'll be hard for him, too.

My excitement grows as each hour passes. I'm really looking forward to our date. Usually the day passes in a flash when I'm at work, but not today. I can't keep still, and Parker looks like he's struggling too, because we aren't getting nearly enough done to finish this project on time.

Sitting back in my chair, I can't take it anymore. "What do you want to do tonight?"

He grins widely at me but doesn't say anything, just watches me.

"Did you change your mind?" I ask hesitantly, afraid he's going to say yes.

Releasing a deep belly laugh, he stresses, "There are many things I want to do tonight. We agreed on dinner, but we can see where it goes."

A sigh of relief envelops me. I do want to get to know him much better, and I really want to pick up where we left off. "Good, what time are you thinking?"

"I made a reservation for seven at Capannina on Union. How does that sound?"

I've heard good things about the restaurant. "Very good. Meet you there?"

"No. I'll walk over to your place, and we can grab a rideshare over."

"Looking forward to it. Now we need to get a little bit of work done." I'm doing a happy dance in my mind. I can't wait for tonight.

The afternoon creeps by; when it finally hits five, I begin to pack up. "I think we'll need to work on this over the weekend."

"You're probably right." He steps in and whispers in my ear, "You distracted me all day today, and I didn't get anything done." My hand grazes his crotch on accident, right across his semi-hard cock.

I smile at the thought that he's as aroused and excited about tonight as I am. It's been ages since I've had a proper date.

Texting Tonya, I ask: **What do you think I should wear for my date with Parker? We're going to a nice Italian restaurant close to the house. And don't suggest the pink micro minidress.**

Tonya: Well if you want to get laid, that dress will do it.

Me: I have to be able to look him in the eye at work next week. No micros or even minis. I want some mystery.

Tonya: Okay, okay! What about that pretty pastel green floral sundress with casual sandals.

Me: That sounds like we're in the right ballpark. Good idea. What if it gets cold?

Tonya: Snuggle up to him.

Me: What if he picks his nose and I don't want to snuggle up with him?

Tonya: If that's his worst sin, you're in good shape.

Me: Ewww.

Tonya: Grab your cream-colored sweater, or don't you have a pashmina scarf?

Me: Black pashmina. I'll go with the cream sweater.

Tonya: Put your hair in the big hot rollers for soft curls and wear just a touch of makeup.

Me: Hurry up and move here so you can help me dress for these occasions in person rather than over text.

Tonya: I'm working on it. Have fun, and text me when you get home.

I'm just putting my lipstick on when the buzzer rings. "I'll be right down," I announce into the speaker.

"May I come up first?"

Normally if a guy asked to come up to my apartment on our first date, I'd consider telling him I didn't feel well, but it's Parker, and I'm excited for tonight. "Sure, apartment 2B."

He arrives with a beautiful bouquet of white roses. "I hope this isn't too much. You look beautiful."

I've rarely had people compliment me, so I'm sure I'm twenty shades of pink. Taking the bouquet of flowers, I'm amazed by the blooms. "They're gorgeous." I step in and kiss his cheek. "Thank you."

I finally notice what he's wearing, and butterflies take flight in my stomach. He fills his khakis out perfectly, paired with a nice pair of loafers, and I know he's a man's man when he wears a stunning pink button-down shirt with the sleeves rolled up. He looks so handsome.

"A rideshare should be downstairs in a few minutes."

"Let me put these in water and we can go. Thank you again for these, they're stunning."

"I thought that, given all the help you've provided me and to celebrate our first date, they were perfect."

I go into the kitchen and put the roses in a vase of water. Stopping to wipe my sweaty palms on a kitchen towel, I take a big breath and then walk back into my sparse living room. He's standing at the balcony door, looking out over the street. When he sees me, he smiles broadly. "I think my place has the same layout as yours."

"So many of these places were rebuilt after the 1998 earthquake."

As we walk down the stairs to our waiting rideshare, he asks, "You were here during the earthquake? What was it like?"

"My mom and I were living in an apartment over in Chinatown. The World Series was going on, and I had just come home from school. We were in the living room talking about what I'd been doing that day in kindergarten. Then there was a big rumble, and everything shook. I just remember thinking a big truck hit the building—which happened another time when it was delivering to the store on the street."

"How did you realize it wasn't a truck?"

"I guess because my mom grabbed me and held on."

"Sounds like she was terrified."

"She was. We had several aftershocks, and once they calmed down, we went outside. It was crazy. The entire front of some buildings fell off into the streets, and I remembered thinking they looked like giant dollhouses. We wandered around and tried to help people when they needed it and just surveyed all the damage. There was a freeway that used to run around the Embarcadero that collapsed."

"That must have been crazy."

We arrive at the restaurant, and once we're seated, we talk about the differences between his hometown of Seattle and San Francisco. It's relaxing and fun, and we enjoy the evening.

Dinner is outstanding, but the company is better. I've never felt so comfortable with a date before. When we do hit lulls in conversation, I never feel like it's awkward or I need to fill it with mindless banter. We're not in a hurry to finish our meal, but after dessert and coffee, it's time to head home.

He rubs his hand back and forth over my arm as he sits next to me in the rideshare, an erotic touch that I feel at my very core.

Kissing him chastely on the cheek, I smile and tilt my head. "I'm not ready for tonight to end. Would you like to come up for a drink or something?"

"Or something."

My heart races and my stomach swirls with excitement.

As the driver turns on my street and takes us the last three blocks, my excitement mounts. "Are you ready for this?" I whisper.

Picking up my hand, he puts two of my fingers in his mouth, gently sucking them while looking at me intently, sending an electric current straight to my core. I'm visibly aroused and weak in the knees.

Looking me in the eyes, he says, "I was an Eagle Scout. I'm always ready and prepared."

If I thought we could have privacy, I'd probably do him here on the sidewalk. Dizzy from the magical chemistry between us, I try to maintain my composure and walk to the front door of my building.

As I unlock the building's front door with my key, his hand finds my backside and caresses my ass. I turn, and he sheepishly whispers in my ear, "I was just wondering if you were going commando under that dress."

Without a word, I turn on my heels and walk up the stairs to my apartment. I can feel Parker's eyes on me as he follows.

In my nervousness, I fumble and drop my keys. He picks them up and unlocks the door, then steps aside to usher me in. Instead, I shove him ahead of me, pushing him against the wall before the door even closes behind us. Sucking on his lower lip before our tongues meet in an aggressive tango. I greedily reach for his belt, wanting to see what's been teasing me all night. His pants fall to the floor and he steps out of them.

His mouth's perfect, as is the rest of him. I drop to my knees, removing his hard and wanting dick from his pants. I always thought he might be hung, but once it springs to life outside of the confines of his pants and boxers, I'm stunned.

"It's so big," I murmur before taking him deep in my mouth, sucking up and down while looking at him. I flatten my tongue so I can take more of his length deep into my throat, flicking at the tip when I pull back up. I cup and massage his balls with one hand while holding his cock steady at the base with the other as I work it in and out of my delicate mouth.

Fire spreads through my veins—pure, hot, unadulterated lust. God help me, I want him.

It doesn't take long before he warns, "I'm going to come," but I don't stop. He shoots his load deep down my throat, and I just keep going, swallowing every last drop before I pull back.

"Fuck, girl. You're incredible," he exclaims as I stand up in front of him, smiling as I wipe at my wet chin.

He steps forward and grabs hold of my ass with both hands to raise my feet off the floor. I cling to his shoulders as I direct him to my bedroom, where he throws me on the bed before lifting my dress. He traces his tongue up my leg to my black lacy thong. I'm sizzling hot and can't take much more, and then he dives between my legs slipping my thong off and tossing it over his shoulder. He inhales deeply and spreads my lips, running his tongue along the side of my clit. I moan my appreciation and he reaches beneath my lace bra for my hard pink nipples, rolling and pulling them between his thumb and forefinger.

Gently, he sucks the hard nub into the warmth of his mouth, and I lose myself in a sea of emotions. My head falls back, and my hips move with the rhythm of his tongue. He applies pressure to my swollen clit, circling it over and over as he inserts a finger and rubs at my G-spot. Grabbing his hair, I moan my encouragement for him to keep going. Pulling on my sensitive nipples and moving my pussy as if I'm fucking his face, I climax with a glorious full-body shudder.

The franticness of the buildup of our evening slows, and we both take our time to undress. My breath catches as he peels his shirt off. It's like he was etched in stone. His chest's perfectly ripped with a flawless six-pack beneath it. He has a slight sprinkling of curls between his pecs, and I can't wait to run my fingers through them, then down his happy trail until I find the treasure at the end. And he smells so good. I think it's sandalwood, but scents aren't necessarily my expertise. I only know what I like, and I like him.

He joins me on the bed, and we rest for a short while without really talking. He pulls me in, and I lay my head on his chest, touching him, caressing the tight curls on his chest and rubbing him, coming up just short of his cock which is bobbing and begging for my touch. We just lie together in a surprisingly comfortable silence.

His cock grows harder and harder, and when it seems he can't take it anymore, he rolls me over on my back and I stare deep into his eyes. Removing a foil package from the side table, he sheaths a condom on his hard and anxious cock. Watching, I lick my lips in anticipation.

"You're so beautiful when you lie there watching me."

I spread my long legs wide, and my hips move in an attempt to capture his cock as he rubs it up and down my slit, teasing me.

"Please! Please, I can't take this torture," I beg.

Leaning down, he suckles each of my nipples, teasing them with his tongue and mouth as he finds my wetness and barely brushes his thumb over the swollen nub. I moan at the contact, but I can't take it—I need and want more.

He thrusts hard into me and we both gasp at the intrusion as I struggle to take in his length.

"You're so fucking tight," he gasps as he slowly and deliberately drives deeper inside of me. I wrap my legs around him, adding weight to every thrust.

He feels incredible, and I'm in ecstasy.

Once I've adjusted to his size, he starts to speed up, the erotic sound of our bodies slapping against one another filling the room. My tits shake with each pounding, begging to be played with. It's almost as if he can read my mind, as he leans down and bites my nipple. The sting doesn't hurt, but he groans as my core clenches him even tighter.

He maneuvers to a kneeling position and commands, "Show me how you play with your clit when you pleasure yourself."

I strum the hard nub with three fingers as he plunges inside me at a rapid pace. I feel the wave of my orgasm building, my breathing becoming labored, and I start to moan.

"That's it. God, you're beautiful. Come for me, baby. Come for me."

My pussy grips his cock like a vise as I climax, and he groans and joins me in my bliss only a moment later.

After sliding the condom off his flaccid cock, I wrap it in tissue from the bedside table and set it on the floor. I don't want to leave him, even for a moment. This just feels right.

We're both exhausted, and we fall asleep with him holding me tight. I don't typically care to share a bed with my lovers. In the past I've asked them—nicely, of course—to leave after sex, but I want more of him and need to rest a bit.

chapter

NINE

PARKER

THE SUN STREAMS IN THE WINDOW and wakes us.

Last night was intense and amazing at the same time. We make love again, slow and deliberate, and she falls back asleep. I watch her as she cat naps; she's so beautiful and peaceful.

Her eyes flutter open after a while, and I ask, "What do you want to do today?"

"Mmmm. More of what we did last night and again this morning."

I lean down and kiss her. "What else would you like to do?"

"Something I've always wanted to do but never had anyone to do it with would be the Pinball Machine Museum in Alameda. We could explore there and then have dinner at the Indian restaurant I told you about when you decided you liked Indian food."

"I was a jerk. You don't get that you're so beautiful that I get tongue-tied around you."

"Oh, is that what you call it? You weren't very tongue-tied last night." She reaches for my balls and starts massaging them.

I sigh with pleasure. "I love how horny you are, and I love the idea of the Pinball Machine Museum and Indian restaurant. I should run home and grab a shower and change of clothes, though." It's torture leaving her like this, but I have to.

"That would work. And maybe you can pack an overnight bag and stay again tonight? That's if you want to, of course."

I lean down and suckle her nipple, her face contorting in pleasure. “I was hoping you’d ask.” I look over at the clock on the bedside table. “How about I pick you up at one?”

She glances at the clock and agrees. “Do you have a car?”

“I do. It isn’t anything fancy, but I do have one.”

“I’ll be out front at one, then.”

We make out for a bit longer, and then I sigh. “I need to go or I won’t be able to be back here on time to pick you up.”

She walks me to the door completely naked. She’s beautiful, and I love her confidence in strutting her stuff.

“I’ll see you in a little over an hour.” I kiss her and let my hand wander. She’s wet again, and it’s difficult to pull away.

“See you soon,” she says breathlessly.

Thad’s at the apartment when I get there. “I see you got lucky last night.”

I don’t acknowledge his crude comment. “I’m going to shower and head out. I don’t know when I’ll be back.”

“So I guess that means you’re not going out with us tonight?”

The “us” is a bunch of drunkards who came out here from Chicago. “Nope, not tonight.”

“Have fun. And find out if she has a friend.”

I nod as I race to my room and pull clothes together for tomorrow. I debate if I should pack for Monday. I don’t want to spend another night away from her, but I don’t want her to feel like I’m moving in either.

Wearing jeans, an Illini T-shirt, and a pair of grubby white Vans sneakers, I pile everything in my Nissan 370Z. It’s what I call a poor man’s Porsche. I love it though, and we’ll have fun today.

I drive up right on time, and she’s waiting for me. She looks beautiful in white skinny jeans, a blue-green floral top, and some high-heeled sandals, and her hair is pulled back. She definitely gets my engine running. “Nice car. So much better than my ten-year-old Honda Accord.”

“I traded an Accord for this. I don’t drive it much, so having the Honda probably would’ve been smarter.”

We punch the address to the Pinball Museum into the GPS and head over the Bay Bridge.

“Have you been to this place before?” I ask.

"My dad and I came here years ago. He played and I watched."

"Why didn't you play?"

"It still takes quarters, and I didn't bring any."

It doesn't make sense that he wouldn't have given her a few quarters to play. That's strange.

Walking into the museum, I'm stunned. There are over four hundred working pinball machines. Some date back to when they were first built in the late 1800s.

We play game after game, and Constance kicks my ass every time. "I didn't realize I was dating such a pinball machine pro."

"Luck. Pure luck," she teases.

After playing for almost three hours, we work our way to the Indian restaurant. Taking a seat, we're offered two water bowls. I'm not sure what to do, and I almost think it's water to drink until Constance leans in. "These are for washing your hands."

Dipping my fingers into the water, I follow what she's doing. "I've never eaten at this authentic of an Indian restaurant before."

She speaks a few minutes to the owner, and it's obvious that they know each other.

"You must come here often," I say once the owner walks away.

"My mom worked here years ago after my dad disappeared. If they hadn't hired her and given us a room above the restaurant, we would've been living in our car."

"Wow. Why didn't your dad pay child support? Couldn't they find him?"

"He was difficult to find, so they couldn't serve him papers. Robie owns the restaurant and had a big crush on my mom, but it never worked out. I'm very fond of him and love the woman he married. They have five kids now."

"Wow, that's a lot."

"He's happy. He's going to bring us his suggestions for our meal. I did tell him we were both fans of lamb masala, so he knows to include that." Constance promises, "You won't be disappointed."

Dinner begins with the most amazing vegetable samosas I've ever had. The creaminess of the potatoes with the peas in their deep-fried wrappers topped with mint and chutney are melt-in-my-mouth delicious. Constance moans her appreciation and I can't help but stare, picturing her beneath me as she makes those sounds.

She smiles, and I keep admiring her.

"I know I'm not a grocery item, but I can tell you're checking me out."

I chortle. "You want to play that game?"

"Let's see how long you last," she challenges me.

I love this. She's pretty quick, so I might lose, but I'll have fun trying. "How about we play Winnie-the-Pooh and I get my nose stuck in your honey jar."

She giggles. "You've proven to be a master at that, so I'm good with you being stuck in my honey jar. How about this one: Trust me. It'll only seem kinky the first time." She grins widely, and my dick is hard as a board.

Robie sets a tureen of soup in front of us and explains, "This is shorba, a thick soup with lentils, vegetables, and chicken."

"Thank you," we both say in unison.

Digging into our soup, we start talking about Pineapple Technologies and our project. We're completely immersed in our conversation when Robie removes our bowls and replaces them with naan, coconut rice, chicken tikka, lamb masala, and palak paneer. It's not as crazy a meal as I expected, and I dig in like a starving man.

She looks over at Robie fondly as he works. "He brought all my favorites."

"It's great that you both are friends." I can't help but continue the naughty innuendos. "I'm on top of things. Would you like to be one of them?"

"Yes. Do you know karate? 'Cause your body's really kickin'."

Leaning across the table, I growl, "What time do you get off? Can I watch?"

"I think you've already done that. Do you like jigsaw puzzles? Let's go to my place and put our pieces together."

I'm running out of these stupid lines, but it sure is fun to run them back and forth with her. "If you were aspirin, I would take you every four to six hours." She's laughing hard, and I love it. "What has 142 teeth and holds back the Incredible Hulk? My zipper."

"You win! I surrender!" she says through her deep laugh.

"You'll surrender to me tonight."

God, she's funny, beautiful, and smart. I'm so lucky.

We barely get the door closed before our hands and mouths are all over each other. She touches the bulge in my pants, and I make a little whimpering sound, eager to lose my clothes. As I rub her breasts against me and she caresses my cock through my pants, a smile spreads on my face.

"Your belt looks extremely tight. Let me loosen it for you." She smiles at me seductively and bites her lower lip.

After a few more moments of our intense making out, I'm already hard. That has a lot to do with our dinnertime flirting and our intense kissing and groping, but I'm harder than usual, stiff with the thought of enjoying my Constance again.

Quickly I regain my composure, lifting the dress off her body and exposing hard nipples poking through the delicate lace of her bra. Her breasts fall nicely above her firm stomach, covered slightly by her glowing cascading hair. I see the wet spot on her panties, and my heart skips a few beats knowing she's as turned on as I am. Pulling my pants off, I stand in all my glory and enjoy her look of desire as she gasps.

I squeeze my cock and a bead of precum forms quickly at the tip. She leans forward, her tongue flicking out to lick it off, but I pull away.

"Oh please?" she pleads, grinning.

Then her lips are around me, her tongue exploring the tip of my cock. She looks up into my eyes, seeking signs that the warmth of her mouth on me is having the desired effect. Which, of course, it is.

She bobs slowly on my erection, her lips gliding up and down, coating me with her saliva. We both gasp and moan, completely unfeigned pleasure. For a short time, she looks up at my face as she sucks. I stare down into her eyes, savoring the moment.

After a few minutes of her sensuous oral ministrations, my body quivers as she pulls up again. When she starts sucking with redoubled effort, I shudder again. "I'm gonna come."

I moan as a long stream of cum erupts from my cock, followed quickly by a second smaller spurt. She continues to suck with abandon, wrestling third and fourth surges from me. I'm breathing heavily as I reach down and run my hand through her hair. She's still sucking me slowly, gently, draining every drop from my shaft.

"Oh yeah, that's sooo fucking good," I pant.

She slips my cock from her mouth and looks up at me with a smile, then presses her lips against mine. I open my mouth to kiss her in a sensual embrace, our tongues dancing together hungrily, seductively. Her heaving breasts grind against my chest, her nipples hardening and poking at my own.

I kiss my way down her neck, suckling gently on the fleshy spot where it meets her shoulder before continuing down her body. As I hover over her tits, she reaches under me to cup them together, rolling her nipples gently between her fingers for me as my mouth opens to take one in.

Hungrily I engulf a breast, my lips plaster around the pert nipple. Her body shakes slightly with a soft sigh of pleasure as my tongue flutters over the erect nub in my mouth. I release it with a trail of saliva stringing down to the nipple as I exchange it for the other one to do the same. I watch in delight as her fingers knead my saliva into the nipple I just left.

After partaking in the feast of breasts that I could've only imagined would be that perfect, I make my way farther down her body, trailing my tongue down her belly and over her navel.

She watches as my head lowers, but then her eyes close as the waves of pleasure hit her when I plant my tongue in her folds. I press lightly into it, swirling and circling over her pussy lips before sliding up and down over her slit, working to part her lips and expose her fully to me. Her hips begin to rock, swaying to the rhythmic caressing of my tongue. Soft whimpers billow out of her with each pass of my tongue until I stop and look at her pussy glistening before me, the succulent lips being held apart by her moist fingers. Her sighs and moans tell me to dive back into it.

Watching her give herself over to me with the confidence of a woman who is secure in her body makes my dick hard as a rock.

In and out my tongue fucks her swiftly as her hips rock in time, fucking my mouth right back. She starts to whimper, whispering things to me to urge me on. I try to listen, and I try to oblige. I place my mouth over her swelling clit, lips pursed around the throbbing rosy nub, and her shriek of delight makes me lust for more as two of my fingers snake their way inside.

She's closer than ever. She grips my hair tightly, tugging at me and thrashing my head side to side before allowing my free hand to slide up her body and knead her tits together.

And then it happens.

Her mouth drops open wide, waves of pleasurable cries spilling out into the air as her body shudders, wave after orgasmic wave making her body tremble as she flows onto my fingers while my tongue flutters against her clit. I withdraw my fingers, dripping wet with her climax, and suck them into my mouth.

"God, Constance, you taste so good," I whisper as I lie next to her trembling figure.

Her eyes finally open to meet mine and she rolls on her side to face me, a look of pleasure and lust emblazoned on her beautiful face as she gazes at me and smiles.

I've never been a possessive guy. Not ever. Not until Constance. Now I want to protect her, make sure she's always happy and safe. Maybe I've been able to tap down those instincts in the past, but my protective streak toward her is so damn strong now that I've been with her, touched her, been inside her sweet body.

She's mine.

chapter

TEN

CONSTANCE

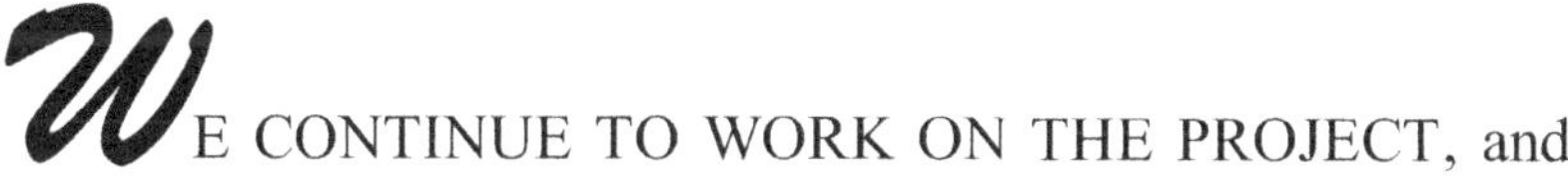

E CONTINUE TO WORK ON THE PROJECT, and I'm covering for the new receptionist when the front desk phone rings.

"Hi, Constance, this is Tony downstairs. There's a Mr. Steve Trades here to see you." He stresses, "You specifically, Constance."

"Thanks, Joey. Can you let him know I can't see him right now and that I'm busy?"

"Oh. Okay, if that's what you want." In a low voice, he murmurs, "You know it's Steve Trades, right? Like the tech guy?"

I cringe internally. Of course I know him. I also hate him. I try hard to hide my irritation that my father has just shown up when I reply. "Yes, I know who he is. You can tell him what I've said. Don't worry about it. "

"I'll do that. Thank you, Constance. I'll tell him and won't let him up."

I continue working away when suddenly Mason's standing at my desk. "Constance, is there a reason that Steve Trades was refused entry into our offices?"

Crap. I'm so mad right now that my dad had the audacity to come to my office. "Well, I was told he came to see me, and I don't want to talk to him."

Mason's eyes widen, mouth gaping. "Do you know Steve Trades?"

I take a breath, figuring honesty is the best policy. "Yes, I know him." *Shit, here we go.* "He's my father."

Mason's breath catches. "Oh! I didn't know that. Th-that is, uh, surprising," he stutters.

It's time to beg. "Mason, I don't mind that you or the partners know, but can you please not let everyone in the office know? I want to make it here on my own. I've never used his last name, and there's a lot of family drama. Ninety-nine percent of the time, he ignores me and I ignore him. I'm not interested in having a relationship with him."

"Well, I'm not about to get into your personal life. If he was here to see you and you weren't interested in seeing him, I'm okay with that. You can send him away." He nods at me. "I promise I won't let anybody know. That can remain our secret."

I'm surprised how relieved that makes me. My secret can stay safe. "Thank you, Mason. I do appreciate that."

He leaves, and the elevator doors open without my allowing entry to a visitor. I'm nervous that my father might have found a way to get upstairs, but it's just an employee with a delivery of a beautiful bouquet of flowers.

"They're for Greer," he says as he places them on my desk. "It was chaos downstairs, so I volunteered to bring them up."

"That was nice of you. I'll let her know."

I dial Greer to alert her of the bouquet. She knows I'm technically not supposed to leave the front desk unless I have some coverage. We've had some security issues, and I have an emergency call button.

As I think about it, if my dad does come up, I would push the button. I don't care if it would make the news.

When she picks up, I say, "Greer, you've just received the most beautiful bouquet of flowers. Would you like me to bring it back in about an hour when our temp returns, or would you like to come up and get them?"

"I could use an excuse to stretch my legs. I'll come up and get them." A few moments later, she arrives with a Diet Coke for me. "You look upset. Is everything okay?"

"Yes, everything's fine. I'm a little frazzled. My father decided to arrive unexpectedly today and wanted access to our offices. It's thrown me off."

"Well, he's welcome to come up. Just because the new security system is here doesn't mean we're refusing entry to anyone as long as we know them."

"Thank you, I understand. I'm just not interested in dealing with my dad at work."

She pats me on the arm. "Oh, I have a mother who's a little crazy herself. Trust me, it'll get better."

After the temp returns from her lunch break, I walk into the break room to grab my lunch. As my leftover lasagna heats in the microwave, I hear, "He was in the building to see somebody."

"Why would he be here? There's no reason for Steve Trades to have anything to do with any of the companies here."

"Do you think he wants to invest, or maybe buy one of the companies in our portfolio? He doesn't work with any of the mergers and acquisitions."

"Are you sure it was him? I mean, why wouldn't a company want to see him?"

"Tina said she heard the security guard called someone and they told him he couldn't come up. He had a fit in the lobby and asked to speak to the owner. Boy, I'd hate to have to explain why I turned him away."

I take great satisfaction that he went to Mason and was still refused. My father isn't getting his way. He's used to people bending over backward for him, and his temper is legendary.

"Holy crap! Who could imagine that anybody would refuse to see Steve Trades? Boy, they must not be getting along. I mean, if he could give me a new phone and computer, I'd see him."

They have no idea. He doesn't give anything away—not even to people who share his DNA.

After lunch, I head back to the conference room. It's exhausting working through this project with Parker. We sit here for almost ten hours a day, every single day. We're about three-quarters of the way through the project, and Parker's getting antsy. He wanted to have this portion of the project done for his meeting the day after tomorrow with the FBI, but it won't be. The code has become more complex, and he's slowing down. I'm working as fast as I can, and I'm actually keeping up with him.

Parker runs his hands through his hair and expels a long breath. "We need to be faster."

"I'm going as fast as you're giving it to me. The pivot tables are here, and we're working it through. What else would you like me to do to help?"

"I don't know," he snaps. "We just need to get this done." I know he's irritated, so I don't take it personally.

"I'm here now, and I can stay as late as you need." I sympathize with him and also want this behind us.

"No, you distract me. It's all your fault that this has slowed down."

Okay, now it's personal. "My fault? What the hell? It has nothing to do with me."

"Yes it does. You and your skirts with your tits out there for everybody to see. It's a distraction for everyone who works here."

I stand up, slamming my palms on the desk. "I don't need to take this from you. My skirts haven't changed, and I'm not putting anything out there for anyone." I drop my voice to just above a whisper. "Just because you sampled the merchandise doesn't mean you have any right to declare what I can do and wear." I glare at him in case he wants to challenge me. "Let's get the rest of this figured out and finished. After we're done, we don't have to talk to each other anymore."

He looks at me like a lost puppy. "That's not what I want. I'm sorry. Um… excuse me."

He gets up and leaves, practically running out the door.

chapter

ELEVEN

PARKER

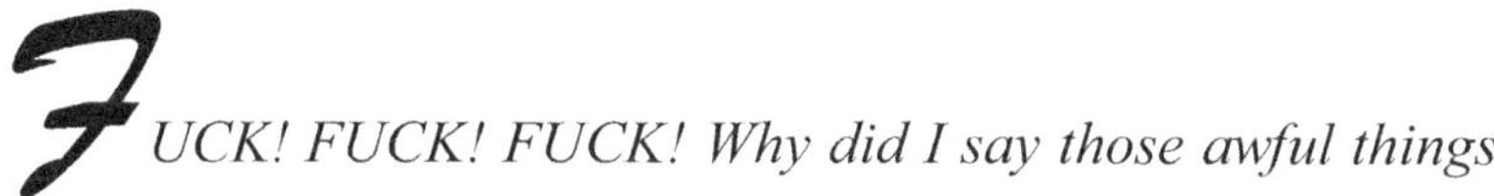

UCK! FUCK! FUCK! Why did I say those awful things to Constance?

That wasn't what I meant. Yes, she's distracting me, but it's not her fault.

She's right. She's absolutely *right. Why did I say that? How can I make it better?*

I grip the sides of the sink in the men's room and stare at myself in the mirror. Good grief, I only want to spend time with her. I want to continue to see her after hours. She's become important to me. I didn't mean to say what I said.

Crap!

How am I going to fix this?

I sleep walk through the rest of my day and leave at the first chance I get. When I get home all I can think about is what I did to screw this all up.

As dusk turns to night and then turn to early morning I lay in bed. I can't sleep, watching the clock turn from one to two to three. I've made a mess of things. I replay the conversation over and over in my mind, thinking of all the things I could've said differently. I didn't mean to make her feel bad.

My phone rings. Glancing at the clock, I see it's shortly after six. The caller ID says it's my dad's cell phone, and my stomach drops. "Hey Dad, what's up?"

"Sorry to call so early." My mind jumps to a thousand places: my twin sister Elizabeth, my grandparents, my dog Fred…. "Your mom and I are here at University Hospital. She's in recovery after having had surgery early this morning."

"What? Why? Is she okay?"

"She was in a car accident last night. A drunk driver swerved in her lane and hit her head-on." I hear him begin to choke up.

"Oh God. Is she going to be okay?"

"Parker, your mom had a punctured lung they repaired. She still has some broken bones that need to be set by the orthopedist," he manages to get out.

A drunk driver? What was she doing out? She drives a safe car, eats healthy. She keeps her weight down, she's active. She should never be in a hospital. But you can't plan for car accidents.

Closing my eyes, I hold back tears. My dad's a mess, and I need to be strong for him. "What does that mean?"

"She had surgery to repair the punctured lung early this morning. She's going to have surgery tomorrow or maybe the day after to repair her hip and leg. She'll be in the hospital for several days, then will start an aggressive physical therapy regimen."

"Is she going to be okay?"

"All things seem to point to positive. I don't want you to worry about anything. I'll call and keep you posted."

"Have you talked to Elizabeth?"

"I called her earlier this morning since she's on the East Coast. I didn't want to wake you." He doesn't expand about my sister's plans.

"I want to be there for Mom. I'm flying in. I'll be on a plane today. There are three airports here—one of them will have a seat. What's Elizabeth going to do?" I move to a travel site and start putting up flights to Seattle from the Bay Area. They're expensive, but I don't care right now.

"She's going to try to be on a flight out of Boston this afternoon."

"I'm booking a flight right now out of San Francisco. I'll connect with Elizabeth, and we'll get a rideshare from SeaTac to the hospital. Tell Mom I love her and I'll get there as fast as I can."

My dad clears his throat. "I'm sure she'll feel bad if you come and are disconnecting from your life in San Francisco. What will your bosses say that you're just jetting off home?"

"Dad, that's not the kind of place I work at, and if they did say something about it, I'd never come back. I love my job, and I can work wherever there's an internet connection. I'm coming. There's no debate."

"It'll mean a lot to your mom." I can already hear some relief in his voice.

The flight I booked is at 3:20 p.m.; I'll land by 5:30 p.m. I'll go into the office this morning and get things lined up to work remotely at least for the next week.

Picking up my phone, I call my twin sister. When she answers, I can tell she's been crying. "How are you doing?"

"I'm a wreck. And you?" she whimpers into the phone.

"The same. Dad started to lose it during our call, so I'm going to try to hold it together for him."

She sniffles. "I'll try to do the same. I get in a little after six."

"I get in just before that. I'll try to get to your gate. Let's take a car over together."

"Sounds like a good idea. I'm so worried, Parker."

"Me, too. I'll see you in a few hours. I love you, baby sister."

"Love you, too."

Now I need to alert everyone at work. I know we can never plan these things, but the timing couldn't be worse. I put together an e-mail.

To: Cameron Newhouse, Cora Perry, Constance Hathaway
From: Parker Carlyle
Subject: Family Emergency

My mother was in a serious auto accident and has been admitted to University Hospital in Seattle. I've booked myself on a flight out of SFO this afternoon with a return flight tentatively set in a week. I'll be working from her bedside, and will be available for calls and anything else you may need. I'll be in the office this morning to line everything up.
Parker

To: Parker Carlyle
From: Constance Hathaway

Subject: Re: Family Emergency

I'm sorry about your mom. Would you like a ride to the airport? I'd be happy to take you.
C.

To: Parker Carlyle, Cora Perry, Constance Hathaway
From: Cameron Newhouse
Subject: Re: Family Emergency

Family first. You have a computer. My fiancée's a doctor—granted, a pediatrician—but if you need to talk to anyone who can break down any medical jargon or refer you to anyone here locally, please don't hesitate to ask. We can catch up on the phone later if you need to take the morning.

To: Parker Carlyle, Cameron Newhouse, Constance Hathaway
From: Cora Perry
Subject: Re: Re: Family Emergency

Be safe, and I hope your mom has a speedy recovery. We can let you know of any meetings, and you can video chat in on a secure line—but only if you want to. Cameron's right, family first.
Cora

I decide I'm only going to respond to Constance. I could take a rideshare and not inconvenience anyone, but I need to apologize again.

To: Constance Hathaway
From: Parker Carlyle
Subject: Re: Re: Family Emergency

A ride to the airport would really make a difference. I can come into the office for a couple hours this morning, and then we can leave about lunchtime. I'm

expecting only to be gone for a little over a week, and
I'd love the help to get there.
P.

To: Parker Carlyle
From: Constance Hathaway
Subject: Re: Re: Re: Family Emergency

Not a problem.

I throw a few things into a drag bag. As I'm finishing up, Constance texts me. **I'm leaving now. How about a ride into work, if you haven't left yet?**

Me: Perfect timing. That'd be great.

I walk out a few minutes later as she pulls up. "This is great service. Better than any rideshare."

"I don't know about that," she teases. "My car's not as clean, and I don't have water or mints for you." We both chuckle. "Actually, I wanted to apologize for yesterday," Constance says sheepishly.

"Why are you apologizing? You didn't say anything I didn't deserve."

"It was inappropriate to go off on you."

"Then let me apologize. I'm a jerk. You're not responsible for me being distracted, I am. Please don't change how you dress."

"Friends?"

"I was hoping for more than friends, actually," I admit.

She smiles at me and turns a slight shade of pink. "I'd like that, too."

I head straight for my desk when we arrive and begin going through my to-do lists and outstanding items. I'll meet with Cameron on which files need to be moved to other people and what I can work on while I'm gone.

I look up when Constance puts a cup of coffee and one of the breakfast burritos in front of me. I didn't realize I was hungry until I smelled it. "Thank you. I would hate to miss a breakfast burrito."

"They do go quickly around here. Cameron would like to meet with us in twenty minutes. Will that work?"

I nod. "I sent you a large packet of information for the pivot table."

"I'll get it entered today, and you'll have it when you land in Seattle."

Cameron walks up with his own coffee and breakfast burrito. "Come on in, you two."

We file into the conference room behind Cameron, eating and sipping coffee while we go through what I have on my plate. Cameron isn't taking anything from me, but he insists I leave it all behind.

I'm sure he can see the conflict on my face, as he tells me, "Parker, your family comes first. If you're working, you aren't spending time with them. We'll be fine if these don't move for a week."

My flight arrives in Seattle a little early, and I locate my sister's arrival gate with ease. She's the first person off the plane. We embrace, and she begins to cry. "I'm not ready to say goodbye to Mom."

"I did some research on the plane, and from what Dad described of her injuries, she should be fine," I attempt to reassure her.

We grab a rideshare and take it to the hospital, getting directions to the surgery ward from the front desk.

Elizabeth puts her arm to stop me and affirms, "We're strong. We can do this."

I give her a quick squeeze, and we both take a big breath.

When we enter the hospital room, Dad is sitting next to Mom holding her hand. He's always adored my mom. I can only hope to love a woman half as much as he does. I know without any doubt that he'd step in and take all the pain away from her if he could.

He looks up when we enter and comes over, bringing us into a wide hug. "Thank you for coming. Your mom was so happy when I told her."

She seems to be sleeping soundly, so we whisper to keep from waking her. We sit together in her room until the nurses send us home. "You're not doing her or yourselves any good by sticking around," one of them admonishes.

Dad drives us back to the home I grew up in. The furniture in my bedroom hasn't changed much since I left nine years ago.

I text Constance. **I'm home and will sleep in my childhood bedroom. Is it too naughty to wish you were here?**

Constance: Maybe a little, but I like that about you. How's your mom doing?

Me: She's heavily sedated right now. She has another surgery first thing in the morning, so we'll go over early.

Constance: Let me know if there's anything I can do.

Me: I will. I'll check in with you tomorrow.

Constance: Wish you were here.

Me: Me, too.

I'm exhausted, but I don't sleep very well. After my conversation with Constance, I feel like we can get beyond what I did and get back to where we were, but my mom really occupies most of my thoughts. I even worry about my dad. I'm not sure he would make it if something happened to my mom.

We arrive before her surgery and are able to see her. As they're rolling her in for knee surgery, she wakes up and sees Elizabeth and me for the first time.

"I love you both," she tells us with a weak smile. "It wasn't necessary for you to come, but thank you."

Elizabeth and my dad break down at her words. I pinch the soft spot between my thumb and finger to keep me from crying, too. I need to be strong for my family.

We've been told the surgery could take between two and three hours, so we wander down to the hospital cafeteria, each ordering a greasy breakfast and just moving it around on our plates. Eventually we head back to the waiting area.

Two hours pass, and each time someone enters the waiting area in scrubs, we jump up.

Three hours pass, and my dad begins to pace. We're sitting on the edge of our seats.

Four hours pass, and now we're all pacing. The nurses' station confirms with me that she's still in surgery, and that only ratchets our anxiety higher.

Our family pastor arrives to sit with us. No one wants to leave in case they might miss the surgeon—no bathroom breaks, coffee breaks, or even a snack run.

At four and a half hours in, the surgeon finally comes. We all stand and lock arms, waiting for the news.

"Marjorie's in recovery. The surgery went well. We placed a rod in her femur and eight pins in her left leg. She'll be sore, and we'll need her to be able to do a few things before she can be discharged from the hospital. That usually takes a few days." He turns and leaves before we can figure out if we have any questions.

Elizabeth collapses in a chair and weeps. A nurse comes over and sits next to her, rubbing her back. "He's not known for being Mr. Personality, but he's an excellent surgeon. Your mom's doing great. She's coming out of anesthesia, but she'll be on some serious medications for a while. She won't be back in her room for at least an hour. There's a place that hospital staff like to go since the cafeteria gets old. It's close and fast. You need to breathe some fresh air and get a decent meal."

Numbly we nod and take the address from her, then slowly make our way to the elevators and head over to the restaurant. It's raining a soft, steady drizzle, the smell permeating my senses with a combination of the moss that grows everywhere and dirt. I've missed this.

The food's outstanding, and we eat in silence, becoming energized to stand vigil for Mom.

After our meal, we return to the waiting room and only wait a few minutes before we're told that they're bringing Mom into her room. She's a bit groggy, but she smiles when she sees us. "I hope you didn't stay here and wait for me."

"There's no place we'd rather be," my dad whispers and kisses her on the forehead.

"You gave us quite the scare, Mom," Elizabeth shares.

She frowns. "I didn't see him until it was too late."

"It's not your fault, Mom," I comfort her.

She smiles and drifts off. The nurse comes in and tells us, "She won't be awake for a while. We've upped her pain meds for now, but it looks like they'll start to wean her off them after dinner tonight. Go home. We'll call you if anything significant happens. She needs her rest, and I think you do, too."

Reluctantly we leave and head back to the house. My dad drops us off and heads into his office at the law firm. I know he wants to do the same thing as I do—work to occupy his mind.

I begin to work on Pineapple's code, sending packets to Constance as I go.

An instant message comes up from Cameron. **How's your mom?**

Me: She made it through surgery and is sedated. We'll head over after dinner, so I'm working for the time being.

Cameron: Offer still open if you need any translations from Hadlee.

Me: I'll let you know. She's in the hospital for the next three days, so I'm sure there will be something.

Cameron: Don't worry about Pineapple if you can't get to it. It can wait the week.

Me: It's a welcome distraction, but thanks.

Time moves like molasses in winter. Elizabeth went with my dad to his office this morning so she could do something for a client, and I'm sitting in the hospital room, watching my mom sleep and trying to concentrate on work. The noise of the machines beeping and pumping, assuring us she's still alive, brings me great peace.

My thoughts keep drifting to Constance, so I'm not really getting anything done. I text her to let her know what's going on today, and she replies almost instantly.

Constance: Any cute nurses?

Parker: None who are as cute as you.

Constance: What? Are they all men?

Parker: Oh, you're funny. None of them are male. They're all women.

Parker: Wait! Maybe the one who just came in is a possibility. She's cute for a woman over 50.

Constance: Are you going to ask her for coffee down in the cafeteria?

Parker: Why? I have you at home, and you're perfect.

Constance: Perfect? Says who?

Parker: Me. And that's all that matters. Did you ever take ballet lessons?

Constance: No. Why? Do you want to know if I can do the splits?

Parker: Can you do the splits? That would be hot.

Constance: The answer to your question is no on both accounts.

Parker: Hey, what's your underwear look like today? I need something else to think about.

Constance: Pink demi-cup bra and pink matching thong. Why the q about ballet?

Parker: You're so graceful. But it isn't fair that you're wearing such sexy underwear and I'm not there to enjoy it. I wish I was there to see it.

Constance: Maybe when you get home.

Parker: I'm gonna hold you to that.

Constance: Well you have to come back first.

Parker: Oh don't worry, I'll be back. Maybe I'm coming back tonight if you're going to be wearing sexy pink underwear.

Constance: Wouldn't you like to know? I could've lied and been wearing white cotton granny panties and a cotton bra.

Parker: Still sounds sexy to me.

I look up and see my mom's awake. In a raspy voice, she asks, "Who are you texting?"

I'm excited to tell my mom all about Constance. I know they'll get along great, and I can't wait to introduce them. "I've met somebody, Mom. I want you to meet her."

"I'd like that," she squeaks out.

My dad and my sister arrive, and they brought coffee with them. My mother asks, "Do you think I could have a cup?"

Everybody's thrilled to see her moving around, though she still doesn't look like her normal cheerful self. Her chest is wrapped in gauze, and her leg's in a contraption. We sit with her as she makes it through recovery. She's doing better—not fabulous, but her humor's coming back. My sister chides her about being out so late on the night of the accident.

"I was volunteering at the library. It was only shortly after nine when I left. It happened so fast."

The doctor gives us the rundown of what's going on. It's going to take some work, and it'll be a rough road ahead, but she should eventually make a full recovery.

I ask my dad, "How long do you think I should stay? I'm happy to stick around as long as you need me."

"Same with me," Elizabeth agrees.

"There's not a lot you can do right now. Don't feel strapped here. Go back to your lives and careers and take your mind off all of this. Consider coming back in a couple weeks, maybe spend a weekend with her. I think when she's home she'll feel a lot better."

After the nurses inform us that visiting hours are over, we drive home in silence. I watch the tree-lined road that I've driven a thousand times before with a new perspective. To know that somewhere along the winding and twisting road, a drunk man crossed the line and almost took my mom from us, turns my stomach and has bile rising in the back of my throat.

My dad pulls in front of the house and leaves the car idling. "I'm going to head into the office for a little bit." It isn't surprising. He's always worked hard. I don't know where he gets the stamina to work all night and then be with my mother all day.

Once we get inside, Elizabeth heads to the kitchen, shuffling through the mess of takeout menus. "How does Thai sound?"

I nod. I'm not sure I can eat, but it's probably a good idea to at least try.

While we wait for dinner to be delivered, we both sit at the kitchen table and try to work. I've finished all of the data review and sent the information off to Constance. It's finally complete.

This becomes our routine for the next three days. We're all walking zombies, ready for good news and my mom to return home from the hospital.

"What should we do about Mom? I'm not sure Dad can continue working like this and also take care of her."

I've thought the same thing, but I don't have a solution. "I don't know." I take a big breath and try to organize my thoughts. "It's family first, and Mom is going to need help. I know Dad would do it, but he gets in his own world with his client load at the firm. I guess if I need to move home for a while, I can. I don't know about my job, though." And I'm not sure Constance is interested in a long-distance relationship. that the thought depresses me.

"I agree, family first. You have an amazing job that allows for some telecommuting, but they really need you in San Francisco. I'm a freelancer. I have flexibility and can work from anywhere. I don't mind staying if you think someone should be here to help Mom."

A weight that was pushing down on me lifts off my shoulders. "Are you sure?"

"My friends from school are all coupling up. The Charles River is losing its charm. A change for a short time might be nice."

I pull her in for a warm embrace. "I love you, Lizzy," I tease.

"You know I hate when you call me that, Parky."

"Maybe, but it's certainly better than Lizard Breath."

• • •

She tosses a plastic spoon at me. "I could change my mind, you know."

"And if you really would prefer to go back, I'll stay. Mom is much more important than any job."

When my mom is released from the hospital, we have a nice celebration with pizzas made in the pizza oven my dad put in on the back patio when we were in high school.

Between slices, Elizabeth shares, "Mom, Parky and I have talked about me sticking around to help you over the next few weeks."

"Hey, Lizard Breath." I throw a balled-up napkin at her.

"That's enough, you two," my dad warns, then looks at Elizabeth. "I can do this, honey. You need to concentrate on your job."

"Dad, you can't help Mom all day and then work all night. You need sleep. I'm fine. I can work here freelancing. It isn't a big deal, really," she stresses.

And with that, the discussion is over, and I prepare to return back to San Francisco with many promises of phone and video calls.

As Elizabeth drives me to the airport, she tells me, "I hope I can meet the girl you're so crazy about."

I look at her, startled by her comment.

"I'm your twin. I've known you since before we were born. I see that silly look on your face and all the texting you're doing."

It doesn't surprise me that she knows me well enough to figure it out. "I like her. Actually, I like her a lot. But I hope that isn't why you're staying behind. If it's meant to be with Constance, we can make a long-distance thing work."

"No way. Go home. I hope you can bring her back here in a few weeks. I promise to tell her all the reasons she should run away," Elizabeth teases.

"Oh, you're really funny."

"I promise to tell her the truth—you're a great guy, and no one could do better."

She pulls up to the United terminal. Putting both hands in her lap, she gives me a half smile. We both hate goodbyes.

"I can come back in a matter of a few hours. Don't let the distance keep you from telling me what's going on."

"Promise. Now promise to call Mom every day for the next few weeks."

I salute her. "Aye, aye, madam."

I climb out of the car and grab my bag, then wave and blow her a kiss as I walk into the terminal.

Security has lines twisting and turning, with many anxious people watching the time pass by with the hope that they don't miss their flights. SeaTac is always a mess, so I knew to be early enough to plan for this, but I'd still prefer to be waiting at the gate rather than in line.

When the gate agent finally calls my flight we board, I take my middle seat in the second to last row. At least I can't smell the bathroom. Normally it would greatly annoy me, but I booked the flight less than twenty-four hours before my departure last week; I'm just grateful I got a seat period. I only wish the plane would go faster. I'm too amped up to read and it's too crowded to work; I can't sleep despite trying. Constance is meeting me at her place, and I can't wait to see her.

Finally we land. It seems to take forever for people to exit the plane. It drives me bonkers that I'm watching people who've been standing there for fifteen minutes and they wait until the last minute to grab their bag from the overhead or beneath the seat. I know they don't understand that I'm racing to see the woman I'm absolutely crazy about. They don't realize that I need to see the woman who has captured my heart.

chapter

TWELVE

CONSTANCE

MY HEART SKIPS BEATS when I think of his dark curly hair and his luscious hazel eyes that I want to get lost in all weekend. I want to do a happy dance to show everyone how excited I am that he's coming back.

I had a hard time concentrating at work today, knowing I'd get to see him again in person. It's been fun talking to him over texts and on the phone, and we tried to FaceTime, but the connection at my place kept freezing so that wouldn't work. I offered to pick him up at the airport, but given Friday afternoon traffic is so bad, he's going to take BART into the city and I'll meet him at my apartment.

My cell phone pings.

Parker: I'm getting on BART now.

Me: I've decided to meet you at Union Station. I'm leaving the office now.

Parker: I still want to go to your place first.

Me: That's my plan, but I want to see you.

I'm wearing a pencil skirt with a nice slit up the side, plus stockings with a thong on the outside of the garter belt so I can take it off easily. I have a demi-cup bra covered by a button-up shirt. As I see it, I look super conservative from the outside, but underneath I'm all naughty.

I wait for him just past the platform. He walks out and is looking around, obviously searching for me. The women around him try to catch his eyes, but he doesn't see them, his face lighting up when he spots me.

He picks me up and spins me around. "God, I've missed you!"

"I'm so glad you're back."

We start walking out to the parking area and find a rideshare to take back to my apartment, but the ride couldn't be any slower. It isn't the driver's fault, just the traffic; creeping from one side of San Francisco to the other is hard on a normal day, much less a Friday.

We finally make it and walk in my front door, dropping our things just inside.

"I've missed you so much," I declare, pushing him onto the couch so he can watch while I strip for him.

It doesn't take long, especially when he tells me to leave my stockings on, and we have a fabulous time—and a second, and a third. We don't leave the apartment all weekend, ordering all our food in. I'm satisfied and very happy.

The sun breaks through my curtains, and I love the body heat emanating from him. This feels so right. Today's going to be perfect. I know it.

We get a rideshare to work together and walk into the office. I'm nervous that people are going to figure out we're a couple, but my trepidation's short-lived. We enter the elevator together with two other staff members, and they begin talking to Parker and essentially ignore me. I've never been so relieved to be ignored.

When we get to the office, I head to the conference room and he goes to his cubicle. I watch as our coworkers stop and talk to him. We're a nice family at SHN. I like that.

I walk into the break room to pour myself a cup of coffee and grab a banana and hear two of the girls from sales support gossiping.

"I think Parker got cuter while he was gone last week."

"He's single, too. No one's put a ring on him yet."

"I wouldn't mind trying."

"I bet he's beautiful when he's naked."

I can't listen anymore. I know if I say anything, people will figure out we have a personal relationship, and I'm not interested in becoming the subject of watercooler gossip. I debate picking him up a cup of coffee, but as I think about it, I see Parker walk back to Cameron's office, so I return to the conference room.

My part of the project's getting close to being over. I'm not sure how much longer I'll be sitting in the conference room during the workday, but I don't have much to do today.

I stop by Emerson's office and ask, "Do we want to send the temp home and I sit back at my desk and work the front?"

Emerson looks perplexed. "Constance, we hired Melissa. She's the new receptionist."

My shoulders drop, and I fight the anxiousness that comes with becoming unemployed. Apparently I'm not as good of a poker player as I thought, because Emerson grins at me. "After all the great work you've done on the Pineapple Technologies project, we're promoting you to the project team. There will be a couple of other projects we need your organizational skills and help with. We're thrilled with all of your work and how well you got along with Parker and Cameron.

"You'll have some time to figure out where you want to go within SHN. Cameron would love your further support on the technology team, Greer believes you're a natural in public relations and wants you on her team, and of course, I see you as a good fit for several roles within my team. I'm pretty sure the three of us will be able to keep you more than busy until you decide where you want to work."

"I'm so grateful for the opportunity. I like it here. I can't imagine working anywhere else." My cell phone pings and I glance down. It's Cameron. "I'm sorry, Cameron needs me to come over and sit with him and Parker."

"Go finish up Pineapple with them, and I'll put the next project on your desk."

I walk toward Cameron's office and realize I don't have a desk now that I'm no longer the receptionist. I'll ask her about it later.

Taking a seat at the table in his office, the three of us walk through all of the final lines of code. It's over two million lines, which convert to pivot tables. We discuss the best way to present the tables, trying to capture what will be important to the FBI. I'll give them whatever they need.

"Are you free today to join us at the FBI? We'll need someone who can explain some of these tables and show the various data points to them as they need them," Cameron asks.

I nod. "Of course. I'd be happy to come. I'm not sure I can talk about what's *in* the table though, only what makes *up* the table."

"Well, that's what they're going to want to know, so you'll be great. Let's meet at the elevator banks at noon. We'll have lunch first at a favorite spot of mine close to the federal building, and then we can walk over from there."

I return to my spot in the conference room and find a folder on my chair for the SHN Fall Picnic, an event we put on for our staff and all our clients, plus their guests and families. The party has become quite legendary in Silicon Valley. We've had a carnival, a concert by one of the biggest bands in the world, and an event at the San Francisco Zoo. This is the social event of the year for some, and a party people beg to attend. I'm not sure what I need to do with it, so I put it aside to finalize my tables, then download them on a jump drive just in case the FBI won't allow me to use my computer in their offices.

Cameron orders the rideshare, and as we arrive downstairs, a red Prius pulls up. I'm not sure how he's going to fit with his 6'5, muscular body, but he doesn't fuss or freak out as he scrunches into the front seat. I barely manage to suppress a laugh. He leans the front seat back a bit, and I feel like he's laying his head in my lap. Parker's sitting next to me virtually sideways. It's a tight drive, but thankfully not a particularly long one.

When we arrive, it's Parker who has the hardest time getting out, but I can't blame him. A Prius might fit two of my girlfriends and me, but it's definitely a bit tight for Cameron and Parker.

"This is one of my favorite sushi places. I hope you both like sushi." It's hard to keep up with Cameron's wide stride as he walks quickly across the plaza into a side alley. They're able to seat us right away. I can't believe we actually beat the lunch rush.

Cameron and Parker go crazy ordering all sorts of strange sushi, so I'm self-conscious when I order a tuna roll, a salmon roll, and some unagi. When our lunch arrives, we all dig in and eat a good lunch full of energy for our meeting.

We head over to the FBI building with more than enough time to get through security. I'm shocked by the receptionist. Talk about no personality. She harasses Parker about his driver's license and tells him she's not allowed to let him in if he doesn't have a local one. It seems they've been down this road before.

Parker smiles at her and bats those stunning hazel eyes. "I understand. I fully intended to get it fixed last week, but my mother was in the hospital in Seattle, and I've been out of town. I promise to get it done this week. Would you mind calling Cora Perry and see if she'd be okay with me using my Washington ID one more time?"

She rolls her eyes and calls someone. In a low tone, she explains to the person she's talking to about why Parker didn't get his California driver's license.

We only hear our less than enthusiastic receptionist's side of the conversation. She obviously wants to deny him entry, but she reluctantly admits him in the end.

I'm stunned at how long it takes to access the building. I wasn't expecting to have to check in and get the third degree, walk through metal detectors and an X-ray machine, and then have an armed escort. Then again, they are the feds.

When we exit the elevators, I'm introduced to a pretty short-haired blonde in a dark pantsuit. "Constance, this is Cora Perry."

"Nice to meet you."

She extends her hand. "Thank you for coming. We know it's quite the circus to come to us, but we appreciate your patience."

I immediately feel like I can trust her. She sends off this warm vibe with her quick smile and understanding of the craziness.

She turns to Parker and asks, "How's your mom doing?"

"A drunk driver hit her head-on, so she has some significant injuries, but we're glad she'll recover," he shares.

"Do you think you'll move back to Washington?"

Parker's eyes dart to me, and he's quick to reply. "No, I love my job and my friends here in San Francisco."

"Then if you could, do me a favor and get that new California driver's license so it doesn't upset Matilda to break federal guidelines again."

"He'll get it done if I have to drive him down on my motorcycle myself," Cameron interjects.

I take in the offices, surprised by the wall of computers with green blinking lights, people sitting in a large room with modern desks and multiple monitors. When I think of the picture definition of geek, that's what I see everywhere. So different than I expected from FBI agents. When I think FBI, I think three-piece suits, white shirts, red ties, and shoes that look like dress shoes but can be run in.

Instead, I see men and women in Teva sandals, shorts—even a pair of cutoffs and a tank top—but most people are in T-shirts.

We're escorted into a room with glass walls. There's writing everywhere and pictures of several men, and I realize this is the investigation we're working on. It's much more complex than what we've done. I'm stunned at how our work's such a small portion of the whole.

Cora leads the meeting, and each portion of the investigation's represented. I listen closely and absorb everything like a sponge. When it's our turn, they allow me to connect my computer to the screen on the wall but not their network. Parker takes the team through the various data points in all the code, and I show them through numerous pivot tables.

We're asked multiple questions, and I show the data in a way that allows everyone to see the code through different sorts. Several of the team members get excited by what they don't see in what we've discovered. We all agree there's something else missing, though no one can quite place what it might actually be. We're given our direction for the next meeting, and we begin our trek back to the office.

The elevator arrives, and Cameron holds the door for us to enter. "Constance, you really did an outstanding job. Thank you for your help."

I'm embarrassed by the accolades. "Thanks," I murmur.

"Parker, you did a great job breaking down the code. Now you and I have some work to do to figure out how they got past the encryption." They plan for how to divide the work and move forward, while what Cameron said to me keeps playing over and over in my mind. My mother was always quick to praise me, but my father was always super critical. I'm not accustomed to receiving approval from men.

We return to the office and drop Cameron off before Parker and I head back to our neighborhood and stop at a local bar. We order drinks and my cell phone pings.

Tonya: Are you available to get together tonight?

Me: I'm at the bar around the corner from our place. Come meet us here.

Tonya: Us?

Me: Parker and me.

Tonya: I don't want to intrude.

Me: No intrusion. Come and hang out with us. Have Darren meet us.

Tonya: He found out about my dad and is MIA.

I turn to Parker. "Do you think you could invite someone to hang out with us?" I tell him about Tonya and what's going on with Darren.

"My friend Thad thought she was really cute. I'll see if he can join us."

Me: I'm so sorry. Come anyway and I'll shower you with adoration and love. Promise ;)

Tonya arrives a short time later. I order her a strawberry daiquiri and catch up with her as Parker rests his hand on my leg.

Thad arrives and joins us. "So nice to see you beautiful ladies again."

With most of her daiquiri gone, Tonya has a little bit of liquid courage. "I'm surprised you recognize us. You were pretty wasted the last time we met."

Thad doesn't even bat an eye at her jab. "How could I not remember two of the most beautiful women I've ever seen?"

Tonya giggles as he slides in next to her. It's as if Parker and I are no longer sitting here as they start to flirt mercifully. Tonya seems to forget Darren and chats the evening away with Thad.

Parker quietly tells me about Thad. "It's great to see them both get along. He had his heart broken a couple months ago and is finally interested in getting back out there."

"I completely understand. Tonya's first generation, and her dad's super strict. Her parents don't know she rents half my apartment. Her dad has never let her date, so she's a little boy crazy but ultimately shy."

Parker sits back and grins widely. "I think they'll do well together."

A few hours later, after more fried bar food and another glass of wine for me, Parker walks me back to my apartment. "Do you want to come up?"

"I don't have a change of clothes for tomorrow."

"We can always stop by your place in the morning before we go to work."

He kisses me and my toes curl, my core clenching. I want him to stay the night. I've missed him so much this week.

When we get up to my apartment, I pour us both a glass of wine and snuggle into his arms.

"I really missed you when I was in Seattle," he admits.

"I missed you, too. I've never been to Seattle. Tell me about it."

He describes his hometown while his hands wander around my body, his light caresses feeding my insides.

I unbutton his shirt and can't help but gasp at the beauty of his bare chest. In turn, he slowly pulls my dress over my head, leaving me with a simple pink lacy bra and matching panty. "You're so beautiful," he murmurs.

He lightly touches my arm, and I know what he wants. What we *both* want. I roll over to face him, opening my legs just a little, enough to let him know I want him. He rubs the smooth skin inside my thigh and my core contracts involuntarily as it releases a moist heat before he's even brushed against my sex.

He pulls away and continues to rub my other leg, playing with me as he denies me any direct contact that would give me pleasure. He leans down and gives me a tender kiss, and I want to beg for more, but he moves from my lips to my neck to suckle and lick the way I like. He shifts to a better position on top of me, and I want him inside me. I want him to touch me the way he does so well.

"Please. Stop teasing me. I want you inside me," I beg.

"Not until you come first." He continues to nuzzle my neck and lips, while rhythmically circling my nub. "Come for me, sweetheart."

My breathing becomes labored and I pull my breasts out of their enclosures, tugging on my nipples and leaving my inhibitions behind until my climax rushes over me in wave after wave. I'm spent but wanting more.

Bringing him closer with my legs, I wrap them around his waist. He moves my hands from my breasts, holding one while he kisses the areola followed by a swift lick, as if to test the taste of me on each side of the nipple. He breathes warm air over the wetness, making the nipple bead, and I shiver. He kisses it directly and then sucks as much of my breast as he can into his mouth, his hard cock pushing against my clit.

I sigh my contentment. Being with Parker feels right.

He slides my panties off and a moan escapes from his mouth. Taking his hard cock in his hand he begins to slide it up and down against my pussy until it's slick and wet. He teases me by only entering the head. "You're so tight. I can still feel the contractions from your orgasm."

He plunges into me a few inches, moaning his enjoyment. "I need to put a condom on," he growls. Pulling one from his pants pocket on the ground, he opens it while kissing me. In one motion, he rolls the condom on and enters me once more.

He begins slowly thrusting, and my breathing changes as he hits the spot that will send me over the edge again. Another wave of orgasm hits, and I moan my appreciation.

"I'm going to come too quickly if we continue in this position." He pulls out and turns me over, leaving me exposed. He pushes into my pussy again, his right hand holding the small of my back as his left pulls my hips back to meet his. I moan and push back hard. I've come twice, and I want him to have some satisfaction. His pace increases, and he comes with a groan.

We separate, and he gives me a deep kiss. We hold each other for a few moments and drift into a warm, peaceful sleep.

We wake up a short while later and move to the bedroom, continuing to alternate between sleep and moving from soft and slow to hard and fast, then back.

I look over at him, and I think we're both a little drunk from our orgasms. Thinking about all the fun we've had tonight, I realize we've moved from just hot and good sex to lovemaking, and I'm surprisingly comfortable with the change in our relationship.

chapter
THIRTEEN

PARKER

I'M A LITTLE TIRED AFTER all the exercise we had last night. When I think about Constance in all her glory, it makes me smile. I'm pretty confident that nobody here at the office knows what's going on, and that's the way it's going to be for the time being. She's all mine; I'm not going to share her with anyone.

As I look through the various lines of code, something jumps out at me, but I can't figure out what exactly. It slowed down my evaluation when the code became inelegant. I didn't think anything about it at the time, because different developers have different styles, but now it's sticking out like a sore thumb.

Studying the lines, I realize that every one starts with a different letter. I sit back in my chair and shout, "Holy shit!"

To verify what I think I'm seeing, I walk to the conference room and start writing the first few letters of several lines of code.

"What's up?" Constance asks.

"Just a minute."

I circle the first letter of each line of code and then write it out.

Dillon Cameron and Mason you should have hired me when you had a chance now I will destroy you and all of your investments Pineapple is just the beginning

"Hoooooly shit!" Constance exclaims. "Is that in the lines of code?"

I nod, standing back and looking it over. I want to be sure I'm not making this up.

"Do you want me to get the partners?" she asks.

I nod once more and Constance leaves. I start examining the code again, looking for other clues. Mason, Dillon, Cameron, and Sara all arrive almost at the same moment, and we all stand around the whiteboard.

"You've got to be fucking with me," Mason says in a whisper.

Cameron's looking closely at my work. "How did you see it?"

I explain how it all came together. "It seems to spell it out. Am I crazy?"

"No, I don't think so. That's no coincidence. Do you see it anywhere else?" Mason asks.

"Not yet. I'm sure there's more, I just need to find it."

Everyone's silent as we look at the ramifications.

"Cameron, how about you alert Cora and Jim. Invite them to the Arnaults' on Sunday night, and we can meet as a group." Turning to me, Mason adds, "I think you and Constance should join us."

I nod, and Constance does as well.

The team disperses, and Cameron has me join him in his office, where we conference call Cora and Jim to share our news.

"Can you tell me which lines these are?" Cora inquires.

"It's one hundred and twenty-six total lines beginning at line 400,328."

"That's a catch that would've been hard to find," Cora shares. "Well done, Parker. If you ever get tired of earning your way to be a billionaire, I hope you'll talk to me first. I'd love to have you on my team."

My cheeks hurt from smiling so widely. I've been slaving over this code for weeks, and to finally see a big find. I'm thrilled and over the moon. A little voice in the back of my head tells me I should've seen it earlier, but knowing no one in the FBI or Cameron found it is awesome. I love solving the puzzles that reviewing the code offers, but I think I like the evaluation side over puzzle solving full time. Though working for the FBI would definitely be a fantastic backup plan.

"Hands off, Cora," Cameron responds teasingly.

"You're welcome to come too, Cameron. You both are as strong or stronger than my best developers. Your talents could help us put some real bad guys away."

"Cora, once we get past this, let's sit and see how we can help you guys," Cameron offers.

"Deal."

I spend the weekend working. I don't mean to ignore Constance, but I want to be ready for the partners meeting on Sunday night. She and I agree to go over together; I drive us in my car, and she uses Waze to get us there.

"I'm so thoroughly turned around," I admit.

"I grew up here and am turned around, too. I had no idea that Hillsboro had such an exclusive community," she sympathizes.

We finally get to the house and park, and a herd of excited dogs comes running at us. Constance drops to a knee and is almost licked to death by the pack.

"Billy! Molly! Riley! Heel!" The dogs cautiously break away. I look up and see Caroline Arnault, someone I've seen on television a thousand times, walking over with her hand extended.

"You must be the amazing development team that Cameron's been bragging about. I'm CeCe Arnault."

"Wow," I say under my breath as Constance reaches for her hand. This is *the* Caroline Arnault, and she's heard about us.

"Nice to meet you," both Constance and I say.

"Come on in. We have a taco bar tonight for dinner."

We follow her inside the house, and my stomach growls at the aroma of Mexican food.

We're standing off to the side while everyone visits. I mutter, "Did you know Sara was married to Trey Arnault? How did I not realize that?" I grab Constance's arm. "That means we're in the home of Margo and Charles Arnault."

She starts laughing so loud that people are staring. "You're completely geeking out."

"I totally am. I mean, Charles and Margo founded Sandy Systems. They made much of today's computing possible."

Margo walks into the family room where we're all gathering, and Cameron introduces us.

"Constance?" Margo looks her up and down. "My, have you grown. It's been years. How's your dad doing?"

"I think he's well. I'm surprised you recognize me."

"You look like the same angel you did when you were six." Then she turns to me. "Parker, I understand you're a technical genius like Cameron, and you found a mysterious message in the code."

"Yes, ma'am," I answer.

"Well done. Dinner will be shortly. Emerson's making her signature margaritas, and there are chips, salsa, guac, and queso on the back table. Help yourself. If you need anything, please let me know."

"Thank you," Constance replies.

"I didn't know you knew the Arnaults," I exclaim.

"I don't know them. My father does. You know he works in tech. I was maybe six when I met her. I don't really remember her, but I often met people back then. I could pass them on the street and not realize we'd been introduced before."

"I hope to meet your dad one day."

"He's a jerk. You're not missing anything."

Dinner's fantastic, and I'm overwhelmed sitting next to Charles all night. He has amazing stories, and I hang on every word. I pepper him with questions, and he's great about answering them. Finally I say, "I'm so sorry to be so rude and not allow you to eat. My mother would be upset with my manners."

"What are you talking about? We've had a great conversation. Ask as many questions as you need. We did things a little differently when Margo and I were starting Sandy Systems, but I sometimes think that the basic principles can be applied to modern-day companies when it comes to fixing things."

At exactly eight o'clock, we retire to Charles's office. I look at the pictures lining the walls of him standing with several tech gods: Bill Gates, Steve Trades, Larry Ellison, the founder of Oracle. Pure Silicon Valley royalty. Cora Perry and Jim Adelson, our security guy, join us, and we're at the top of the meeting agenda.

I pass around a sheet of paper with the code that captures the first hundred characters of each line of code and the message, and everyone begins to talk at once. Mason quiets us all down, and slowly I answer how it was found. I'm too embarrassed to say that I didn't see it in the pivot tables Constance put together.

There's a lot of "Holy crap," "Good grief," and "Ohhh shit."

Finally Sara asks, "Now what?"

“There are some other areas where the code loses its elegance, and I’m diving into that now looking for other clues,” I say.

“Let us know if anyone from my team can help,” Cora offers.

After finishing our portion of the meeting, we excuse ourselves and head out. It was so cool to be a part of it all. I’ve heard rumors about meetings the partners have offsite, and now I know how much I’d love to be more involved.

chapter

FOURTEEN

CONSTANCE

PARKER HAS BEGUN WORKING on the next phase of the project, which has left me to work with our party planner for the company picnic. We're going with a beach theme, with food trucks, beach games, sand castle contests, and other various activities. I don't have to do much, other than meet with Tina and keep her in budget. According to Emerson, that's the hardest thing to do. She's a party planning genius, and I'm enjoying working with her.

The week was busy, but I'm grateful it's over. Parker and I have spent most nights together and are developing a nice routine. As we're settling in for a pizza and a movie, the buzzer to my apartment rings.

"I'm not expecting anyone," I tell him. "Are you?"

"Nope, I wouldn't invite anyone over to your place."

I walk to the intercom. "Can I help you?"

"Connie, it's your father. May I come in?"

Holy fuck! "It isn't a good time. Maybe sometime next week."

"I've tried to get on your calendar for almost a month. I need to speak with you."

"Again, it's not a good time. I have company."

"Connie, please. It's important."

I sigh loudly. "Fine, let's get this over with."

I look at Parker longingly. Our relationship's over now. My dad will ruin it completely. He'll be direct and kick him out, and his bodyguards will probably say something, and they'll run him away. He may even pay Parker to go away—he's done it in the past. He's always worried people want to get close to me because of his money. What he doesn't get is that I don't tell people we're related.

Fuck! I want to cry. If he's here to tell me he's divorcing his wife and marrying someone else, I swear I'll find a fork and stab him with it. My mother couldn't take that again.

"Parker, all I can say is that I'm sorry."

"Don't worry about it. I can leave if you want to talk to him alone."

"No, that's okay. Maybe having you as a buffer will help."

There's a knock on my front door, and I debate about not answering it. When I finally do, my dad barges right past me, leaving two bodyguards in the hallway. "Connie!"

Parker's eyes bug out as I introduce them. "Steve, this is Parker Carlyle."

"Honey, you can call me Dad."

"Not really. You were only a sperm donor, after all."

"It's nice to meet you," he says to Parker. Turning to me, he admits, "I know I wasn't there for you or your mother, and I don't really have a good excuse. My company isn't an excuse."

"No, it's not. Why are you here?" I'm not interested in his manipulations. I want him to spit it out and leave.

My dad looks over at Parker. "Parker, is it?"

He nods.

"Can you excuse us a moment?"

Parker looks at me questioningly. I can only shrug and shake my head at my father's audacity. I want to beg him to stay, but Parker's so starstruck, I'm not sure anything he could say would be helpful.

"I'll head to your room," Parker finally says.

"What do you need?" I demand when we're alone.

"Let's sit."

Great. Something's going to break, and the media's going to be all over it. My secret's going to be out. So much for the quiet life I've worked so hard to keep.

He reaches for my hand, and I allow him to take it. "Connie, last year I started to lose my energy, and I wasn't feeling particularly well. It was like I couldn't shake a bout with the flu. I've gone to multiple doctors and have been diagnosed with stage IV pancreatic cancer."

I know he wants me to hug him and lavish him with love and affection, but he's never been of any emotional support and is essentially a stranger to me. I don't know him. He's always done the bare minimum that was required by the courts or demanded by my mother. "I'm very sorry to hear that. What does that mean?"

He chuckles. "You hate me, don't you?"

"No, I don't hate you. I don't know you. I hate what you do to my mother, though. I hate that you denied that I was your child and mostly… well never mind. I'm sorry about your illness. Have you told my mom, or are you asking me to do that?"

"I wanted to tell you first. Then I'll tell her."

"Okay. What's the prognosis?"

"It isn't good. Honey, I was a bad father, and I'm sorry. I don't expect you to forgive me, but I want you to know that I'm giving half of my estate to you and half to Lauren and our kids."

"I don't want your money."

"I know that. That's why I think you're the best person to have it. You can spend it on yourself, your mother, or give it away. It'll be yours to do with as you wish. There are no strings attached."

He pats my leg, and I want to slap his hand away. How can he do this to me?

"I don't want your money. Please do not release my name to the press, or say I'm related to you. If you have any respect for me at all, I'm begging you."

"You could help your mother. This is a life-changing opportunity."

He thinks the media circus and bodyguards are worth the crap that comes from being associated with him. What a fucking narcissist.

"I hope you'll change your mind."

"I won't. If you want my mother to have half your estate, give it to her." I stand, and he does, too.

"I know this may be hard to believe, but I do love you. I've always loved your mother. Anne was my muse and my soul mate. We just weren't made to be together. We're two stars that would burn each other out."

I won't cry in front of him. "When will you tell her?"

"I'm not doing well. I want to see her tonight."

I nod. "I hope you find the peace you're looking for."

"I hope you do, too."

He leaves without another word, and Parker comes out of my bedroom once the door closes. "Why didn't you tell me your dad was Steve Trades?"

"Because of this exact moment." I pace back and forth, unable to look him in the eye, carefully trying to pick my words so he understands. "Because you think he's a god and I'm crazy that I want nothing to do with him or with his money. He treated my mom like shit for years. He'd never let her move on. He denied that he was my father, essentially telling her she was a whore. When I was conceived, they lived and worked together, which means they were within reach of each other almost 24-7. And I have enough issues with my mother and how she allows him to treat her. Now he tells me he's dying."

"I'm so sorry." He pulls me into an embrace and rubs my back. "I'm sorry I turned into a fanboy, and I'm sorry he wasn't the father you deserved."

I pull back and throw my hands in the air.

"He was *never* my dad. He was always just some guy who let me down over and over again my entire life. So rather than reach out to me and offer to hang out, he makes it all about his narcissist self. He informs me that, to make up for being a shitty father, he's going to out me to the world and leave me half his fortune—which, let me be clear, I don't want. I'll never have another moment of privacy again. You see how the Arnaults live? They grew up with this shit. I was his secret hidden in the closet. I'm not a fan of his, and I want nothing from him."

"You have Tonya and me to support you."

I look at him and pray that's true; it's going to get rough, and he's got enough going on that he's not going to want my mess.

He holds my hand, and I take him back to my bedroom. We make sweet, slow love, and I worry that, with all the craziness coming his way, he'll run for the hills and this is the last time we'll be together. Once the media gets a hold of this, he'll get the hell out of Dodge. And if he doesn't, he'll only stick around for the money.

My dad always said people only liked him for his money. Maybe he did teach me something after all.

chapter

FIFTEEN

CONSTANCE

MY MOTHER'S A COMPLETE WRECK, calling me at least twenty times a day crying about my dad. He told her he's leaving me half his estate and that I'll take care of her. I realize that by giving it to me and having me share it with my mom, it's less controversial than giving half to his wife and half to his mistress. They've known each other for years and tolerated one another as long as they didn't see one another.

Thankfully he hasn't said anything in the press like I expected. I've been watching his company, and he's transitioning the helm to his heir apparent. The gossip columns have been noting his absence and his frail-looking health for some time; all I can do is sit back and wait and hope that, while he's "making up for my childhood," he listens to my request.

"Did you hear what I said?"

So far, Parker hasn't pushed me about my dad. He's very close to his own father, and I know he doesn't understand what it's like to be repeatedly rejected by the one person who's supposed to love and support you regardless of any and all imperfections. "Sorry, I was thinking about all I have to do at work."

"I wanted to know if you would like to come with me to Seattle next weekend? My twin sister, Elizabeth, will be there, and my parents have heard so much about you. They'd love to meet you."

I'm surprised by his revelation. "You've told your parents about me?"

"Of course I told them about you. Will you come with me? We won't be stuck at my parents'. I promise to show you some of my favorite places from where I grew up and do some touristy things downtown."

"Um… sure. Why not?" I shrug. I've never been to Seattle, and it would be fun to explore it with Parker. "Will it be raining?"

"Possibly, but fall's usually the best time to go. I'll book the tickets. And to be completely honest, my parents may make us stay in different rooms in their house." He looks at me a bit ashamed. "I guess I should've led with that."

"I think if we were going to my mom's, she'd do the same thing." I laugh at the thought of staying at my mom's place. It's only thirty blocks away, so as long as I live in the city, I can sleep in my own house and not have to stay overnight if I visit her.

Our flight from San Francisco to Seattle is uneventful—as every flight should be. I sit next to Parker, and we hold hands. I've flown only a few times in my life, and it makes me nervous; I think I white-knuckled his hand the entire trip.

Parker's father greets us at the bottom of the escalators as we arrive before his sister pops out and yells, "Surprise!" Parker jumps so high that it has all those around us chuckling. I like Elizabeth already.

"I'm so happy to see you," she gushes as she pulls him into a tight embrace.

"Baby sister, are you trying to become an only child? Scaring me like that's bound to give me a heart attack."

"I didn't realize you scared so easily," she teases.

Their father turns to me. "Hello, you must be Constance. I'm Phillip, and this terror is Parker's sister, Elizabeth."

"It's so nice to meet you both." I smile, their kindness making me adore them already.

When we grab Parker's suitcase from the carousel, Elizabeth asks, "How come Constance has a drag bag for the weekend and you have a three-week vacation suitcase?"

I love watching them spar. I can tell there's an underlying sense of understanding and love.

"Because I don't know what I'll need for the weekend. If Constance wants to go hiking to Mt. Baker, I'm prepared. If she wants to only walk around downtown, I've got that covered. And if she wants to go shopping, I have room to carry back anything she buys, too."

"Are you sure you're the male in the relationship?" she ribs.

"You're funny," I tell her.

"Elizabeth, don't mortify your brother too much. He'll remember the next time you bring someone home, and he's relentless," Phillip reminds her.

"Yeah," Parker growls as he gives her the stink eye, "paybacks are a bitch."

"How old are you?" I ask, and everyone laughs.

We exit the airport and drive over a floating bridge. "This is amazing," I share as I stare out the window.

"Don't be fooled. It only looks like this on calm days. When the waves are high or the weather's bad, you don't want to be on a floating bridge," Phillip reminds me.

"That makes sense," I marvel.

"How's Mom doing?" Parker probes.

"She has her good days and her bad, but she's doing pretty well," Phillip tells him.

"Just prepare yourself. She looks rather frail, but she's smiling," Elizabeth warns.

Phillip exits the freeway after we've crossed the bridge, and we wind our way through the streets before parking in front of a nice home. It looks modest from the street, but once inside it opens up dramatically, and the back of the house is all windows. I'm in awe when I look out and see the water and downtown Seattle through the floor-to-ceiling windows.

"Wow, what a fantastic view." Turning to Parker, I chide, "You didn't tell me you grew up on the water."

"The view hasn't always been quite so fantastic. Our parents renovated after we moved out," Elizabeth informs me.

"That's because without you two bottomless pits to feed, we had money again," her dad teases.

I'm given the tour of the house, and each room's nicer than the last. When we stop at a beautiful room with an Ethan Allen four-poster bed and a beautiful bright-colored quilt, I'm in love.

"This will be your room," Phillip informs me.

"Wonderful. Thank you. This is positively lovely."

Parker grabs me by the hand and leads me to his parents' room to meet his mother. She's sitting up in bed, leaning against several pillows.

"Mom, I'd like you to meet Constance. Constance, this is my mother, Marjorie."

I smile at her. "It's so nice to meet you. Thank you for inviting me."

"Parker talks about you all the time. I can't wait to get to know you. You've made a great impression on my son." She looks at him adoringly.

I blush at the compliment. "He's made a great impression on me, too."

I leave Parker to visit with his mother for a short time, figuring they need the opportunity to catch up without me being in the way.

I walk out to the balcony and take in the view once more. It's quite cold with the small breeze coming off the water, and I rub my arms to warm myself. Parker's father comes up and hands me a coat that's too big but warm, then stands with me.

"This is Lake Washington," he explains.

"Parker tells me you're a lawyer here in Seattle?"

"I am. What do your folks do?"

I give him the practiced answer I've given my entire life. "My father's an entrepreneur and a developer, and my mother's pretty much a free spirit and an artist."

"They must be quite the pair."

"They aren't together. They've kept in touch over the years, but they were never married. I guess I was a modern-day love child."

He's silent a few moments. I didn't mean to make it awkward.

"What do you do for SHN?" he finally asks.

"I'm on the projects team. Like Parker, I met one of the partners inadvertently many years ago, and I knew immediately that I wanted to work for them. My role today is to do whatever they ask. That's how I got to know Parker, working on a project together. I'm also organizing a company picnic that we hold for all of the employees and our clients."

"That sounds like a pretty big party."

"Thankfully we have a party planner who's done this for our company for several years. My role's to be her liaison with the office while at the same time keeping her within her budget."

An alarm on his watch rings. "I need to give Marjorie her medicine. I did put you in your own room, but where you sleep after we go to bed is up to you. We don't want to know." He smiles at me, making sure I know the deal. "Please make yourself at home here. We're glad you brought Parker home this weekend."

He leaves me watching the water lap at the dock and sand below.

I now understand why Parker wants me to have a relationship with my own father. I only wish it was something he was capable of having.

As a narcissist, my father has never been one to think about anything other than himself and his own desires. As his income increased, his paranoia that people were only interested in his money also increased. He was always clear that I was to cover my own way in life; I expect nothing, not even love, from my father.

Parker joins me outside. "There's a cool outdoor ice rink we can go to not too far from here. You up for a little bit of ice-skating?"

"I'm probably as good on ice skates as you would be in a pair of five-inch heels."

He lets out this wonderful deep and hearty laugh, his dimples making my heart flutter. "Good. That way we'll get lots of time together, and I'll get to hold you in public as we skate around the rink."

"I sure hope our health insurance works here in Seattle."

The outdoor rink is busy, even though the weather is far above freezing. Parker grabs his skates, the laces tied together, and drapes them over his shoulder, then hands me wrist protectors, knee pads, gloves, and a scarf. He looks at my feet and digs in his bag, passing me a big ball of socks. Holding hands, we walk to the ticket booth, where he rents me a pair of skates and pays for an hour on the ice.

It's going to be a long hour.

After helping me get into my skates, tightening the laces so my "ankles are stable," he helps me walk to the ice. I feel like the dog with roller skates on its paws. I can hardly stay upright.

Parker shows me multiple times how to stand up because I keep falling, then how to skate forward—which was harder than I expected. I still spend more time on my butt on the ice than skating, but eventually it clicks. I'm not able to do any triple salchows—at least on purpose—but I find my balance, and I'm able to at least go around the rink, although I'm sure it's not a pretty sight with my arms stretched wide and my feet farther apart than my shoulders. There are no easy glides for me.

Parker, on the other hand, looks like a pro as he skates around me, and when it looks like I might fall, he's there to catch me. I'm in awe of him skating on one foot, then on two feet both frontward and backward.

"Were you born with ice skates on your feet?"

"Nope, but I started playing hockey when I was three, and I was on club teams at Illini and Chicago."

"I'm making you look bad." I lose my footing and crash down on my butt. We both get a serious case of the giggles. "Just to warn you, I can take you at pool."

"Swimming? I can do a serious breaststroke."

"No, billiards! I'll take you down with a game of 8-ball."

"Then we'll play men against women tonight with Elizabeth and my buddy Tom. I've known him since sixth grade.

My jeans are soaked from falling on the ice and the cold temperature outside. Time seems to pass slowly, but glancing at the clock over the booth, I see it's been barely forty-five minutes.

Parker wraps an arm around me. "Your teeth are chattering. Let's get you dried off."

"But we have fifteen more minutes."

He helps me off the ice, then sits me down and helps me out of my skates. I feel much better on firm ground.

"I grabbed these clothes from Elizabeth. They may be a little big, but I think they'll fit and you'll be dry." He points to the ladies' room, and I quickly peel myself out of my jeans. I'm not sure if my legs blue from bruises or the cold, but I suspect the latter.

When I emerge from the restroom, Parker asks, "How are you feeling?"

"I'm much warmer, so that's a start."

"Great. There's a soup and sandwich place in walking distance. Any interest?"

"Hot soup sounds perfect."

He holds my hand as we walk over, and my chest swells with excitement and the currents delivered by his closeness. I don't think I've ever been this happy.

In line in the sandwich shop, Parker stands behind me and rubs my arms to help with friction heat. "I'm going to order the grilled cheese sandwiches and tomato soup."

"That sounds perfect."

"Just like you," he whispers in my ear.

We sit next to each other at a high-top table once we have our meal. "This is a meal I eat at home all the time. It's pure comfort food for me," I share.

"Me, too. One day I'll have to make you my special grilled cheese with bacon and tomatoes."

"I'll hold you to that. Today was a lot of fun. Thank you for not being too embarrassed by me."

"Thank you for coming to Seattle. It's fun having you here and showing you all the great places that I grew up visiting and seeing."

He takes a bite of his sandwich and the cheese stretches, part of it landing on his chin. I lean in and wipe it with a napkin. I'm mesmerized by his lips—plump, pink, parted, and so damn tempting. Suddenly the only thing I want is to taste him and disappear for a few days alone.

We finish our lunch and head back to the house feeling a little bit warmer, giving me a chance to put some of my own clothes on.

Parker's sister and his best friend arrive. While finding a place for Parker and me to enjoy one another sounds divine, I'd love to get to know Elizabeth and Tom better.

"We're going to do some serious tourist stuff. Care to join us?" Parker asks them.

"It's been years since I've done downtown Seattle. That sounds fun," Tom agrees.

Piling into a car, we drive downtown. I love the easy banter Tom, Elizabeth, and Parker have. They're great at bringing me into the conversation and including me.

As Tom finds us a parking space, I spot a half-dozen ferries taking people from Seattle to the outer islands. I've never been on a ferry. What a great way to commute.

"I can't imagine living on an island," I mutter more to myself than to anyone in particular.

"I know. It's not as if the hospital is close. Imagine if we lived on an island and this happened to my mom. The ferries stop at night, so you could be stranded here. Maybe you could get a helicopter, or in some cases you can drive, but the drive is hours long," Elizabeth explains.

We walk into Pike Place Market, where people are lined up in front of the many vendors selling their goods. It's stall after stall of beautiful, stunning pieces. I look through the jewelry, the indigenous art, the vibrant pottery, colorful hand-blown glass, fresh-cut flowers, fresh and dry fruits that make my stomach growl, various meats—it's everything and anything I could ever want.

I'm so busy taking in all the glorious objects that Parker has to hold his hand in front of me to keep me from interrupting the fishmongers. They're unloading a van full of freshly caught fish, throwing it from one person to another and chanting. While it's work, it's also a lot of show.

Tom leans over to me with a giant grin and teases, "Close your mouth. You're going to catch flies if you aren't careful."

"This is amazing!" I exclaim.

Once they're done, we go to the fruit stands, and I can't help but take a picture. It's almost a patchwork quilt of bright colors, all delicious enough to eat.

I stop at the flower vendor, admiring a huge bouquet. Turning to Parker, I ask, "Do you think your mother would like these?"

Elizabeth looks longingly at the flowers. "That's sweet, and hydrangeas are her favorite. She'll love them."

I finish my purchase and tell Elizabeth, "There was that beautiful pottery vase at one of the stalls at the beginning. Do you think your mom would like that, too?"

"She would love it, but don't feel like you need to get her anything," Parker urges.

"I know, but I want to." I can't explain to him that it's my way of telling her what a great job she did raising her son.

Tom tells the group, "It isn't a trip down to the Market if we don't stop at the original Starbucks."

"Original? It's here? Why didn't I know that?" I ask.

We get in the long line and order drinks, and I pick up a coffee mug to remember my great day of wandering downtown Seattle. There's no place to sit and enjoy our drinks, so we return to the sidewalk to wander the streets and waterfront.

"We aren't done with downtown yet. We'd be remiss if we didn't do the one thing that always identifies the Seattle downtown—the Space Needle," Parker tells me.

Elizabeth hooks me by the arm. "Today's the perfect day to go up to the top."

We take a rideshare across town so we don't have to pay for parking again, then buy our tickets and take the elevator to the top, enjoying the view.

I take in the splendor of the Puget Sound from the Space Needle's platform five hundred feet above the ground. "Thank you for inviting me to Seattle. This is the first time I've been here. What a beautiful city. It's so green compared to San Francisco. I can see why they call Seattle the Emerald City and San Francisco a concrete jungle."

"I love it here, and I'm glad I can share it with you, but I love San Francisco too," Parker shares as he squeezes my hand.

We take dozens of selfies with the beauty of the city and the Cascades behind us. It's great to put all the stress of Marjorie's accident and my father's drama to the side for a bit.

When we return to the house, it's dinnertime. Parker and Elizabeth pull together a simple dinner of baked chicken, steamed broccoli, and plain rice, something they hope their mother can digest with everything she has going on. She joins us at the table, and I can tell she's struggling being waited on; she's used to doing the waiting on them. The family banter is fun, and it's obvious they all love being together.

"Thank you for the beautiful flowers, Constance. I love them. And the vase is perfect," she assures me.

"It's the least I can do for you having me in your home while you convalesce," I tell her.

Phillip asks, "Remember Little Timmy from when you were in elementary school?"

Both Elizabeth and Parker nod.

"Yeah, he used to pull the ribbons out of my pigtails when I was little. Why?" Elizabeth asks.

"Well, he has an interesting invention that he's working with our intellectual property team at the firm. You might want to look him up if you were looking for any investments here in Seattle," Phillip responds.

"What's the area he's working in?" Parker asks.

"He's apparently built a bullshit meter," Phillip announces with a straight face. I can't tell if he's kidding or being serious. "It'll have a way to evaluate a person's voice, like a lie detector, and—"

"Oh, so with this new meter, does that mean he'll cut all the crap you're dishing out right now?" Parker didn't fall for the trap his dad set, and the entire table is laughing.

"How did you guess?" He grins.

Marjorie's laughing, and we're enjoying the levity.

"You thought you could get one by me, didn't you?" Parker tells his dad, then looks at me and winks.

"Nah." Phillip's smiling from ear to ear. "I didn't think you'd catch on quite so quick, though."

"Well, my big brother wasn't born yesterday. Maybe the day before, so he might still be one light bulb short of a chandelier," Elizabeth piles on.

"He does get his brains from his mother," Marjorie points out.

I think this has been my favorite part of the day. I wish my family was something even remotely close to this. They obviously care for each other deeply.

On the return flight home, Parker asks, "So, what do you think?"

"That I missed out on having brothers and sisters and a real family," I share wistfully.

"Family is what you make it. Yours may not have been as conventional as mine, but it was still a family."

"My mother's one of my best friends, and I wouldn't trade that for anything, but my dad regularly did a number on her, and I was often the one taking care of her."

"I know your dad was far short of perfect, but my dad was building a law firm. He was busy and working long hours when we were growing up, and my mom was stuck raising us. She gave up her career for my dad and for us."

"She's pretty awesome."

I don't want to put a damper on our great weekend, but I get the feeling that he romanticizes my father. I know most of it comes from his public persona, but he needs to understand why forgiving my father isn't a quick thing to do.

"You're close to your family, and I understand that it's difficult to comprehend my relationship with my father, but let me tell you what happened on my tenth birthday. I invited twelve friends from school to come over, and we were going to have a party at my house. My father called earlier in the morning, and my mother reminded him that it was my birthday. He decided he wanted to take me out for my birthday, but the only time he was available was during the party that I had planned with my friends. My father didn't want to be with any of my friends, so he made me cancel my party, just hours before it was to happen. I was in a beautiful dress, and my mom had already decorated the house. I was disappointed to not have my friends come over and celebrate, but at least my family was going to be together. We waited five hours for him. My dad never showed up. That day he left me with no party, no friends, and no father."

Parker's eyes widen. "That must've been pretty rough."

"It was, and that's only one example of the dozens of times he let me down repeatedly. It wasn't fair for my mother or for me. It was difficult to watch him marry his second wife. My mom waited for him, never got married to anyone else. One day he came to visit her, and they had a great day together. The next day the gossip columns covered his big wedding to Lauren in his backyard with over a thousand guests. He never told her he was getting married, and I wasn't invited. My mom was devastated. She didn't get out of bed for over a month. I had to call my aunt Jeannie because we were out of food and my mom had no money in her wallet. It took her almost a year to get out of her depression. I called Ruthie, my dad's secretary, and told her what was going on, and some guy showed up a few hours later with a big check.

"My aunt convinced my mom we needed a fresh start. They always liked Hawaii, so Mom decided we'd move there. He never told either of us what was going on with him. We got updates from the gossip papers about his life. It was difficult to hear about him and Lauren having kids. They never invited me over to meet them. We were an afterthought. And honestly, I'm not sure my stepmother and half-siblings wouldn't say the same thing about my dad. He never thought about anybody other than himself."

"You have every right to be angry. He was busy building a company and wasn't around for his family. He's also clearly dying. He wants to make it up to you and spend time with you. If you don't take the chance to tell him how he hurt you, you'll carry it around for the rest of your life."

He may be right, but my father's sucked up so much of my time with anger, hurt, and fear for so long, I'm not sure I care about him anymore. I don't think about him. I don't do anything to appease him or impress him. Instead, I just view him like he is…a sperm donor.

chapter

SIXTEEN

CONSTANCE

MY THOUGHTS FALL TO Parker regularly. We've spent every night together since we returned from Seattle, but I'm not in any hurry to become more than boyfriend-girlfriend; I'm enjoying the get-to-know-you stage, being friends with a little bit of steamy on the side. He's doing a lot to help me get over my trust issues. He's there when he tells me he's going to be, and I know if I were to call him and tell him I was stranded in another city, he would drop everything to help me. He can give me just a look and I get all hot and bothered. I don't know what it is about the attraction, but I need to restrain myself when it comes to him. I'm falling for him, and I'm falling hard.

My calendar's really full today, and I need to get my mind off Parker. When I got up this morning and he was in my bed naked with the sheets wrapped around his torso, the peaceful look on his face and his handsomeness made me very content. I can't stop thinking about him.

Throwing myself into work, I spend the morning with Tina walking through the site of the beach party. It'll be fall, so the temperatures will be cool but hopefully fog free. The water in this area is entirely too cold to go swimming, but we have some great games planned along the beach. I take copious notes and will meet with Emerson this afternoon to walk her through everything so she's comfortable with Tina's decisions.

Riding in the car back to the office, I think about Parker. I love those dimples and his tousled dark-blond hair. When my cell phone pings, I smile that it's him.

Parker: Hey, what do you wanna do for dinner tonight?
Me: Something easy. Anything sound appealing to you?
Parker: As long as I'm with you, I can eat anything.
Me: Yes, you sure have proven that a few times. LOL.
Parker: Aren't you a naughty girl today? Maybe we should cut out of work early for a little bit of fun?
Me: Don't we have to do something with Pineapple Technologies today?
Parker: Yes, way to ruin my evil plan. We're meeting at 3 in Cameron's office.
Me: I'm on my way back. See you then.

Sitting down with Emerson, I walk her through the plans for the fall picnic. "Baker Beach will have parking issues for those who don't live in The City, so Tina has set up the rental of these parking lots"—I point to three large lots on the Presidio—"and she's arranged for shuttle buses that will run every fifteen minutes."

"Great idea."

"We have fifteen food trucks that will be stationed here at this end of the beach. Baker is a public beach, so we can't prevent anyone from walking through our party, but she has some inventive ways to give some of our more popular attendees their privacy."

"Great."

I hand her the itinerary and all my notes so far, including the budget.

"You're doing an amazing job. Well done, and thank you for taking this off my plate."

"No problem, but once you look at the budget, you'll see Tina's about 10 percent over."

Emerson smiles broadly. "We always cut the budget to her by about 12 percent knowing she can't keep to it. Tina knows we have money, and we want a great party, so she can go a little overboard."

"You're very clever."

"She's a lifesaver and does an amazing party. We're lucky she does this for us."

After a quick trip to the bathroom and grabbing a Diet Coke from the fridge, I find my place in Cameron's office, where Parker's already seated. Looking around while we wait for Cameron, I take in the state of his office. It's incredibly neat but cluttered at the same time; filled with papers and books all in various disarray around the room, there's an element of organization to it that makes it still seem neat.

Cameron comes in with a cup of steaming coffee and throws down several chocolate bars. "Help yourself. I think chocolate helps me think better."

Who can argue with that logic? "Thanks." I grab a KitKat and sit back.

"Okay, you two, let's figure out where we are in this clusterfuck." Cameron looks at me and blushes. "Sorry."

"I'm pretty sure I've heard a swear word or two before." I smile at him.

Parker starts going through various points on the Excel spreadsheet and they get technical quickly, most everything flying right over my head. I'm asked to make changes to some of the tables, move them around, and show different points of interest. I'm able to follow that Parker has about one hundred thousand lines to go before he's done with this level of interpretation.

Parker studies the sheet and tells us, "I know there's an anomaly in these last few thousand lines, but I can't figure out what it is yet. There's something bloated in the code, and I'm convinced it's embedded and is important. We need to figure out what it could be trying to tell us."

Cameron shares, "I've been talking to some of the other technology folks across the valley, and we're meeting with the FBI next week as a group. Do you think you both can join us?"

I nod, and Parker adds, "Of course. Happy to be there."

Our meeting wraps up a little before four o'clock, and we head back to my new desk outside Emerson's office. Glancing at my missed calls, I see my father's name listed several times. He hasn't left a message. I figure if it isn't important enough for someone to leave a message, then it isn't worth my time.

My phone vibrates in my hand. He's relentless today. I answer knowing no matter what he says, I'll regret it. "Hello?"

"Sweetheart, I'm downstairs. Please let me up." No pleasantries or even a greeting. Fuck him.

"Sorry, Steve, I'm busy. I'm paid to work, not listen to you. I'll try to schedule something with your admin in the next week or so."

"Sweetheart, it's important that I speak to you this afternoon. Please let me come upstairs."

I don't need this in my life.

"I don't think you understand. I have no interest in talking to you at this point. Maybe I'll get there one day, maybe I won't, but you can't make me listen to you." My anger's building because he isn't respecting my request for space. "I'm working. I don't need you interfering with my life. You've never cared about me before, so leave. Me. Alone." I hang up the phone. I'm sure I'm the only person in his life who tells him no. I'm not interested in the argument any longer, and I'm not giving him another minute of my time today.

I return to the few tasks I need to take care of for Greer, a quiet descending upon the office that doesn't hit me until I hear his voice standing above me. "Constance, please give me a few minutes of your time today, and then I'll get out of your hair."

I stand, not wanting him towering over me, and I see every eye in the office staring at him. I hear whispers of "Steve Trades is here in the office" and "How does he know Constance?"

"How did you get up here? I specifically told you I didn't have the time or the interest to meet with you and you couldn't come up."

"Connie, I'm not going to ask again. I'd like to have a private word with you."

Everyone's standing at their desks and watching the drama unfold. As discreetly as possible, I say in the most menacing voice I can muster, "I'm going to call security if you don't leave."

Standing behind my father is Parker. The level of betrayal hits me like a brick. "Did you let him in?" I fume.

"He called me directly. I didn't know how to tell him no," he pleads.

I take a few deep breaths to get my anger in check. "It's easy—you just say no."

I'm now the center of office gossip. I want to run and hide from the firestorm I know is going to come my way, the fake friends and bullshit I've gotten my entire life when people figure out who my father is. They only see his public persona, where he's everyone's friend and a great guy who sells them handheld computers and phones. They don't get that he was only a sperm donor, that he probably cares more about them than he ever did me.

"Fine, you two can have each other. I'm done with all of you." I give Parker an "I hope you die" look.

Mason has walked over at some point during the scene. "Is everything okay?"

I'm on the verge of tears. I want to run. I don't want to be here listening to my father tell me something that will only affect my mother. I don't want to hear my coworkers tell me how my father has changed their lives in all these positive ways while he ruined mine.

I want to be far away from here. I need to go and go now.

Turning to Mason, I say the only thing that comes to my mind. "I'm so sorry, but I can't do this anymore. I can't be here. I'm sorry, but I quit. Please forgive me."

I pull my purse and bag from my bottom desk drawer and ignore everyone talking to me at once. Dropping my badge and keys on the reception desk, I run out of the office and don't look back.

Parker runs after me. "Wait! Constance! I'm sorry. Please understand, I felt like I was in a bad spot. I only want you to have the chance to tell him what you need to tell him."

The elevator door opens and I step in, then turn back to shove my finger in his face and say, "How dare you? I have told you exactly why I don't want to talk to him, and you ignored everything I said. This is such a betrayal. I don't want anything to do with you if you can't manage to understand that."

When I get outside, I take a deep breath of the San Francisco air. I can't call my mother; she'll only take my father's side. I see a cab passing and I flag it down, give the driver Tonya's work address, and sit back. The tears flowing heavily down my face, I'm a complete mess as I text Tonya.

Me: I'm on my way over to your office. Please tell me you're there???

Tonya: I'm here. What happened? Parker?

Me: Yes, and my father.

Tonya: We'll head to my parents'. Security will keep anyone we don't want away. I'll also order pizza and ice cream.

Me: I love you.

• • •

I cry the entire way to her office. My father has disrupted my life yet again. If he had just sent a message, I could've responded. But no. We meet when and where he wants. Fuck him. And fuck Parker and everyone else who thinks he's a good guy, because he's not to the people who love him.

When the cab drops me at the front of the busy office building, I see Tonya's Mercedes SUV parked up front. She meets me and throws her arms around me, and the tears really start to fall as I just keep asking, "Why?"

She practically carries me to her car, comforting me the whole way. "It's going to be okay."

"I quit my job—the job I loved."

"We'll find you another one that's even better."

Tonya's the best friend ever. She doesn't push me, just lets me wallow in my anguish and the loss of everything at once. It's my fault, but I felt backed into a corner and I knee-jerked.

When we arrive at Tonya's parents', her mother rushes over to me and speaks to me in Mandarin. I have no idea what she's saying, but then she gives me a big hug. "It's going to be okay. Your pizza's here, and ice cream's in the freezer."

"Thank you, Mrs. Wei."

She wipes the tears from my eyes. "You're welcome here always."

I change into a pair of Tonya's pajamas, and she giggles when she sees me. The bottoms look like I'm wearing capri pants and the arms are three-quarter length. "Who buys custom tailored pajamas?" I implore.

"If you had to buy in the children's section, you'd understand." She grabs my hand. "Come on. Let's eat some pizza and watch some chick flicks."

I'm on autopilot. I eat my pizza and a few bites of my Ben & Jerry's Glamfire Trailmix ice cream. I left my cell phone in Tonya's room, not ready to face it, but she's been on hers texting away all afternoon. I know part of it is work, but most of it's me.

"Thad asked if you were with me. I told him you were, and he could tell Parker. But I did stress that the security here at my parents' was pretty thick, and they most certainly were not to come over."

I nod.

"I might have also suggested that he tell Parker to delete your phone number."

I look at her then, a bit alarmed.

She shrugs. "Well, he hurt my best friend. If you decide to like him again, I will, but if you don't?" She pretends to spit on the ground like an Italian grandmother. "He's dead to me."

"Why did he have to do that? Why did he have to take my father's side?" I've been asking that through my tears for hours, and I can't cry anymore. I finally remember crawling into bed and sleep restlessly.

Lying awake, I check the time and see it's after three. The battery is in the red on my phone, so I dig a charger out of my bag and plug it in, then begin the process of listening to my messages. I have almost sixty. Each time I hear Parker, I delete it without listening. There are a few other from former coworkers who are a little too excited because they know who my dad is now. I delete those, too.

Then there's a message from Emerson.

"Constance, first please accept my apologies that your dad was admitted into the building after you expressly told him he wasn't invited. We're addressing the failure in communication. But I won't accept your resignation. You're an important part of my team. Take whatever time you need, but we want you back here when you're ready."

I wipe the tears away. How can I ever work there again and not be the center of all the gossip?

I few more messages from Parker, and again I erase them. Then I get to a message from Greer.

"Well, I heard you had quite the afternoon. Sweetie, you're an important part of this team. We've all had drama in our lives, and it endears you to us further. Please don't quit. I can set you up at home with some work if you'd like. We need you."

I chuckle at her message. I know her mom had a break earlier this year shortly after I started with the company, and it was very hard on her.

More Parker messages that get erased. Then I hear one from Mason, which is very formal.

"I've spoken to Mr. Carlyle. I apologize that security allowed him up after you explained your wishes previously. It won't happen again. I can only imagine how difficult the fuss that people make about your father. We want you back. You're a valued member of our team. Please take whatever time you need, but please come back to us."

"Are you okay?" Tonya says groggily.

"I'm sorry. I didn't mean to wake you."

"Don't worry about it. How many messages did you have?"

"Over sixty."

"Your phone mailbox can store that many?"

"Yes. Steve once tried to reach me and my mailbox was full, so he had the phone carrier set it up. He always wants to be able to reach me, although he never leaves a message."

"Asshole."

This is why Tonya's my best friend. "My thoughts exactly. I had messages from several of the people I work for at SHN, and they tell me I can have my job back as soon as I'm ready."

Tonya sits up and wipes the sleep from her eyes. "That's great news."

"Maybe. They also allude to Parker getting in a lot of trouble for allowing my dad upstairs."

"Good. He should have. I hope he called to apologize for what he did."

"He left all but about ten of the messages. I didn't listen to one of them, just erased them. I also erased the messages from my sleazy coworkers who now want to be friends because of my dad."

"Parker is *so* dead to me."

I chuckle. "What about Thad? If you two get married, Parker will probably be the best man."

"We aren't quite talking about marriage at this point."

"Well, let me be clear. I'll be your maid of honor, and if anyone thinks they can take that job, I'll take them down."

"Don't worry. It'll only be you. I love you, sweetie, and I'm sorry about what happened."

"I know. Me, too."

chapter

SEVENTEEN

CONSTANCE

I'M NOT SURE HOW LONG I've been here. The days are running into one another as I sit in Tonya's room and watch television all day, still wearing the same mini pajamas.

I call my mom once a day, and she rambles on but doesn't understand why I feel the way I do. She likes to tell me, "Your father loves you."

If he loved me, he would've been there for me.

I'm devastated by the betrayal and disappointed by Parker. It's as if my heart's being ripped from my chest. It hurts that he doesn't understand that not all families are as wonderful as his. And mine is definitely not a functional family.

Tonya's parents are fantastic to allow me to hide in their home. Her mother brings me breakfast, lunch, and dinner each day right to my door. She always talks to me in Mandarin, though I know she speaks English fluently with almost no accent. Over the years, I've begun to figure out what she says to me when she speaks Mandarin. I could never fathom speaking back to her, but she's extremely kind to me and has been the only mother figure in my life, since I was the mother to my own.

Leaving a tray on the side table next to the bed, she puts her hands on her hips and shakes her finger at me, lecturing me in Mandarin.

When she finishes and looks at me questioningly, I tell her, "Yes, Mrs. Wei. I know, I'm not doing myself any good moping around here."

She has a satisfied smile on her face. Continuing her Mandarin verbal assault, she then gives me an encouraging hug and mutters something I can't quite hear.

"I'm sorry. I'll take a shower in a bit," I tell her.

She heads to the door and observes in English, "Your Mandarin's improving."

"Not really." I give her a forced smile. "I'm guessing you're just saying what I'd say to someone in my condition."

Thinking I'd better check in with the world, I rummage through my things and pull out a charging cord, watching a rerun of *Gilligan's Island* and picking at the split ends in my hair as I wait for my phone to come to life. In every episode, they think they're going to be rescued, and they never are. How do they manage the disappointment? And why is Mary Ann always the person cooking? I hope someone else does the dishes.

I'm watching the giant spider corner Gilligan when my cell phone pings, signaling a text.

Tonya: Check out the newswires. Your dad's all over them.

I click on one of the links she attached and see pages of articles, but that isn't surprising. He founded a global company. I'm even mentioned—though not by name—on his Wikipedia page.

I click the *Wall Street Journal* link, which says my dad's sick. I look at several news sites from across the world, finding most of the real newspapers are speaking about what the impact of his relinquishing the helm of his company will be while he spends his last time on this Earth with his family. I snort at the thought. *Asshole. You didn't want to spend time with us before. You think God hasn't noticed?*

The tabloids approach the gossip about his public feuds with former friends, the board of his company, and talk of the size of his estate. The comment about the estate is what raises the hair on the back of my neck. I know that shortly the tabloids are going to show up on my doorstep. I'm comforted knowing I'm far away in Palo Alto, avoiding the chaos that's going to quickly come my way.

Tonya walks into her room and stops short. "Honey, I love you, but you stink. You need to take a shower and get dressed."

I mumble, "I can't. You saw all the newspaper articles announcing my father's stepping down from his company because of his illness. The craziness is going to descend. We talked about this over a decade ago."

"I know, and it seemed so far away at the time. Have you talk to your mother?"

"Yes, every single day. She's not taking my dad's impending death well. She keeps blubbering about him like he's a saint."

"Do you know if they're talking?"

"I think so, but not as much as she'd like. She'd prefer to move in with him and take care of him, but of course Lauren's already living with him, so that wouldn't work. I think Lauren's patient with his long-term affair with my mom, to a point, but I can't imagine she'd want to share the same house with her."

"I think we need to go out. Get some fresh air, enjoy a few drinks, maybe meet a boy or two and check on the apartment."

"Any boy you want to see in particular?"

She grins. "Well, there's the six-foot blond-haired god."

"I don't want to see Parker."

"I promise no Parker. Only Thad and a few of his other friends."

"I'm okay to go back to the apartment. I'm beginning to understand your mother's Mandarin, and I'm becoming a burden."

"You're not becoming a burden. My parents don't mind, and in fact, my mother kind of likes having someone to take care of. I'm thrilled that they're focusing on you and not on me."

"You and Thad are getting a little hot and heavy. How's that going?"

"Well, he hasn't taken my V-card yet, if that's what you're asking."

The V-card is a sensitive subject for Tonya. Her parents have always wanted a nice Chinese boy from the right family for her, and they've pushed for her to remain a virgin. She's ignored all their meddling in her life, but that's where she's stayed the course.

"Whenever you're ready. Don't let him rush you into anything you don't want to do."

"I know. I can't bring myself to go there quite yet, but God, can that man kiss, and his fingers are magic."

I love the sparkle in her eyes and her excitement. My current predicament is putting a real damper on her fun, and I don't want that for her. Placing my fingers in my ears to plug them, I repeat, "La, la, la, la, la. I don't want to know your personal life. I'm okay not knowing anything about your sex life."

She giggles. "Well, there isn't much of a sex life, but that's okay. I've packed up my overnight bag, and we're going to get you dressed."

It does feel good to have the pounding hot water pouring over my aching muscles. I dress in the suit I arrived in—which of course Mrs. Wei sent out to be dry-cleaned. They spoil me.

Wrapping my hair in a messy bun, I say goodbye to Mr. and Mrs. Wei, giving them both hugs and kisses.

"You come back if you need to get away, or if you want some good Chinese love," Mrs. Wei yells after me.

"Thank you. It means more to me than I can say. If it gets too bad, I'll be back. I appreciate having a place to hide."

We return to the quiet apartment, and I grab the pile of mail—mostly junk—and toss it on the counter, then drag myself back to my bedroom. The sheets are still rumpled from Parker. My heart aches and tears immediately spring into my eyes. Sitting down on the corner, I start to cry. I miss him, but I'm not ready to forgive him. I may never be.

Tonya gets dressed for her date with Thad in a simple light blue dress and cute flat sandals. "You look amazing," I tell her.

"Thank you. Are you sure you don't want to go out with us?"

"I'm positive. It wouldn't be much of a date with a third wheel."

"Are you going to be okay here alone?"

"Of course. I'll miss your mother feeding me, but I can do this," I say with more confidence than I feel.

Thad rings the buzzer and comes upstairs. "How are you doing? Parker's torn up over what happened."

"What did he tell you?"

He holds up his hands. "Nothing really, only that he fucked up big-time."

I nod. I don't want to cry in front of Thad so he can tell Parker what a wreck I am over him.

"He's been trying to get a hold of you."

Tonya whips around and exclaims, "His numbers have been blocked. He's not allowed to talk to her after what he did to her."

"I'm not trying to get in the middle of it, I only wanted to ask how you were doing. I'm sure he'll ask once he realizes I saw you."

"You're welcome to forget that you saw me so you don't put yourself in that awkward position," I grumble.

Quick to defend me, Tonya warns him, "He hurt her needlessly, and she's not interested in having any further conversation with him."

"He got in a lot of trouble at work," Thad volunteers.

"As he should have," Tonya impresses upon him.

"I'm going to be fine," I announce so they can get on their date before I screw up their relationship over my mess.

They reluctantly leave, but I'm grateful for the time alone. I sit in the apartment as the sun sets and it begins to get dark. There's solitude in the white noise of the busy streets of San Francisco outside my window—no television, radio, or anything else.

I keep going back to Thad telling me that Parker got in trouble at work. I can't care about that, but I'm curious as to why. He's the golden boy and I can't imagine that the incident with my father would get him in trouble.

The downstairs buzzer rings, bringing me out of my reverie. I hope Tonya didn't get locked out.

"Did you leave your keys?" I ask over the intercom.

"Miss Hathaway?"

"Who are you looking for?"

"Constance Hathaway, the illegitimate daughter of Steve Trades. Is that you?"

"Sorry, you have the wrong apartment."

"I'm from the *Star Journal,* and I was wondering if I could ask you a few questions about Steve Trades."

"I don't know what you're talking about. Go away." I let go of the button, and a sourness rises within me, making my stomach churn. I think I'm going to be sick.

They found me. Fuck.

My apartment's dark, and though I want to turn a light on, I worry it'll encourage anyone who's found me to stick around and try to get in.

I need to warn Tonya.

Me: The tabloids are here. Be careful when you come back.

Tonya: Do you need me to come home now?

Me: No. Have fun and enjoy your evening with Thad.

Now for my daily call to my mom.

"Hi, Mom. I just had the *Star Journal* ring my buzzer to talk about Steve. They may be headed in your direction, so you may want to go to your sister's up in Mendocino."

"They've camped out on my front step already. I don't know how to get out of here." I hear the anxiety in my mother's voice, and it isn't a great place for her to be. This could send her into depression, and I always worry she may do something foolish.

"Mom, don't trap yourself in the house. Please go see your sister. Get away from this mess. They can't trespass on her property, and since she's so far off the road in a deeply wooded area with the gate closed, they can't get close enough to take any pictures."

"I think I'm stuck here. I should've left last week as soon as the news broke."

"I'm calling the police and telling them you need an escort out of your home because you don't feel safe."

"I don't want to be on the news. That'll upset your father so much."

Part of me would love to have his nasty little secret out in the open for all to see, but I guess he did that when he broke the news. Asshole.

"I know how you feel, Mom. Someone rang my doorbell, so they're on the hunt for quotes. Go to Aunt Jeannie's before it gets worse."

"What are you going to do?"

"I may go back to the Weis'. I'm not sure yet." I can tell she's undecided. It could get worse, and when I was younger, we talked about this. "Mom, I'm calling the police. Pack your bag and be ready to go."

In a small voice, she whimpers, "Thank you, sweetheart. I love you."

"I love you too, Mom. Take your cell phone and only answer if you know who's calling."

"That's a good idea. I'm sorry," she mumbles.

"Mom, you always told me, 'You can't help who you fall in love with.' Remember that. I'm hanging up now."

I call 911 and tell them reporters are trespassing on my mother's property and she's scared and can't leave. They agree to go help, and I'm relieved knowing she can get away from this mess.

Jeannie was never a huge fan of my dad, but I should still let her know what may be coming her way.

She answers after the sixth ring. " Jeannie? It's me, Connie."

"Hey, sweetie. I heard the news. Are you and your mom okay?"

"I'm fine, but Mom's trapped in her house. The police are going to escort her out and probably to the Golden Gate if they're worried she's going to be followed."

"She knows the code to the gate, and I'll tell Burt at the sheriff's office to make sure only your mom gets through."

"Thank you. She sounded upset."

"She called me last week and was crying over his diagnosis. I'm convinced it's karma and he got what he deserves." She's silent for a beat, then adds, "I'm sorry. I don't mean to be so cold. I… I'm sorry."

"It's going to get worse. He told me when he was first diagnosed that he's leaving Lauren half his estate and me the other half."

"Holy crap. Really?"

"Guy hasn't had any interest in me for twenty-five years, and now he's going to die and leave me in a shit storm."

"Oh, sweetie. I'm sorry."

"It's going to devastate Mom that he didn't leave anything to her, but he wants me to take care of her. I'll set up a generous trust for her and give the rest of it away."

I hear my landline ring. Nobody ever calls me on that phone, mostly because I don't give the number out except to family or on a job application. I let it go to voice mail, figuring even though it's an unlisted phone number, the press knows no bounds and would have no problems figuring out how to get to me.

"You're good to my baby sister," my aunt soothes.

"She's my mom, and I love her. Thank you for allowing her to hide with you."

"Of course. And there's plenty of room for you when you're ready."

"I appreciate that."

My mom calls moments after I hang up with Jeannie. "The police are here. Do you want to come with me?"

"I can't come right now, but I talked to Aunt Jeannie. She's waiting for you. Burt, the sheriff, will be at the gate to make sure no one follows you in. Use your code."

"I hope I remember it."

"It's my birthday. Do you need me to text it to you so you have it? I know this makes you nervous."

"No, the day you were born was the best day of my life."

"I love you so much, Mom. Be safe, and do what the police say."

"Love you too. I'll call when I get to Jeannie's."

Popping a bag of popcorn in the microwave, I sit cross-legged with all of the lights off, listening to what's going on outside. I hear only the traffic as I eat my popcorn and drink a Diet Coke. When I peek out the window, I see a few people standing around, which isn't normal.

I don't know what to do when my landline rings again. Crap! I'll need to unplug it quickly. When I pick up the phone and hear the notification for a voice mail, I stop and listen to it. There are six messages.

The first is Sara Arnault. "Honey, it's Sara. I'm calling with my husband, Trey, and his sister CeCe. We're here, and we're thinking about you. We've been through this, and we want you to know that we're here for you, and if we can help in any way, don't hesitate to ask. If you'd like to get away, let us know. We have a hideout up in Stinson Beach, and you're more than welcome to join us. Please call us back and let us know you're okay." She rattles off a phone number and hangs up.

I listen to the next voice mail. "Constance, it's Emerson. I want you to know that Dillon and I are here, and we'll come in and get you if you need help getting out of your place. I'm familiar with your neighborhood, and I know the alleys, so we can lose any paparazzi. We can figure out where to go next. We live in a doorman building, and you're welcome to stay here anytime. The doorman will keep them away, and they'll never know where you're staying."

I sit back and cry listening to these people. After I quit so abruptly, they're still so good to me. How did I get so lucky to work for them? Everything my father touches that's not work-related he burns it to the ground, and it turns to ash.

My landline rings again, and I cautiously answer. "Hello?"

"Constance, this is Caroline Arnault. I'm an advisor to SHN, and Sara's my sister-in-law. We met a few weeks ago at my parents'?"

"I remember."

"I'm so glad. I've reserved a private room at Quince tomorrow night. We can get you there under the radar. Let's get together and have a talk, get some food in your stomach, and we can help you strategize on how to manage the chaos that's raining on you right now. Greer and her fiancé will be there, along with Emerson, Dillon, and Mason. I promise we'll get you out in front of this so you're in good shape, and maybe the press will leave you alone. We care about you. Please consider meeting us at Quince at seven o'clock tomorrow night."

My buzzer keeps ringing. "I guess I can be there."

"I hear the buzzer going crazy. Do you need a place to stay tonight? I'll come get you."

"No, I'll be okay. I'm sitting in the dark, so they'll give up eventually."

"Let me know if you change your mind. This is my private number." She rattles off a number that I barely get written down. "We'll see you tomorrow at Quince."

I can't decide if this is a weight being lifted off my shoulders or if I've just walked into the tiger's den.

My door rings regularly until about one; someone must have done something that disconnected it. Tonya has checked in with me, and I've warned her to stay away. Hiding in the corner of my bedroom, I try to get some rest.

My decision to leave is easy but hard to put in place. It's before dawn when I pack an overnight bag and pull my hair back, then call a rideshare to the airport. I'm not going anywhere, but it might prevent someone from following me.

I walk through the garage in the dark, making my way to the corner where I've made arrangements for the rideshare to meet me three blocks over. I greet the driver and slink into the corner of the car. I keep looking at the traffic, but with only being able to see headlights, I can't be sure anyone is following us.

"You running away?" the driver questions in a thick indiscernible accent.

"No, just heading out of town for a few days to get a break." I don't want to tell him the truth for fear he'll be all over the tabloids talking about where I'm going and that I was scared.

He drops me off at the United departures, and I walk into the airport like I'm headed somewhere. I spot a Starbucks before security and get myself a coffee, then hide in the corner far away from anyone. No one looks in my direction, so I'm cautiously optimistic.

I notice the *New York Times* and the headline announcing my father's illness. Below it are pictures of me, and Lauren and her kids splashed across the front. It's not the local newspaper, so that means this information is most likely the cover of all newspapers and tabloids. I've become media fodder, and it's disconcerting. I used to be able to walk down the streets and no one knew my name; now pictures of me are all over the place. A guy I knew in high school's quoted in an article about me and how he met my father—which is all untrue. I'm not sure there's any place I can hide.

Four mocha frappucinos later, it's getting close to lunch and I'm Starbuck'ed out, and ready for a change. I've been debating my options, and I think it's time to ask for help. Calling Emerson, I tell her I'm in hiding and ask if I can come by.

"We'll pick you up and bring you in through the garage. Where are you exactly?"

"I'm at the airport. I can take BART into town and meet you somewhere."

"Nonsense. We'll come to you. Dillon and I will be there in thirty minutes. Let's meet upstairs at departures. It's a little less crowded."

"Thank you," I whisper.

"No need to thank us. This is what friends who understand do for one another. We'll be there soon."

As I get up to leave, a young woman approaches me. "I didn't want to bother you, but I wanted to tell you how sorry I am about your dad."

Crap. "Thank you." I walk away and find a hiding spot, standing between a wall and a window.

I watch Dillon and Emerson drive up. They have a beautiful beagle for me to share the back seat with. "I'm sorry to screw up your Saturday morning," I tell them.

"Did you try to get out of town?"

"No, but I thought if the press believed I was leaving, they might leave me alone. And if they didn't realize it was me, it was a neutral place to meet."

"You're a natural spy," Dillon says, obviously impressed.

"I don't know about that, but last night I needed to call the police to help them get my mom out of her house and on the road up to Mendocino to stay with her sister."

"That sucks," Emerson scoffs.

During lunch at a bistro, a man wearing a Trades War shirt—one of the retail outlets for my father's stores—approaches me and blubbers, "Your dad's a hero."

Dillon stands. "Thanks, man, but can you give her some space? She's grieving, too."

In a full cry, he sobs, "I just love him," before he walks away.

"This is going to be my life," I murmur.

"I had no idea." Dillon shakes his head.

"I met Bono when I was fourteen on my father's boat. Bono fawned all over him. This is his world, and I've always hated it because he gave them everything and gave me nothing."

I'm exhausted when we return to their apartment, a beautiful loft in Pacific Heights. It's modern with an elegant touch, and it makes me want to be Emerson when I grow up—having it all together, a hot husband, and a job I love.

I hide in the guest room until it's time to leave for Quince, hating to inconvenience everyone. I wear a black sheath dress and some pretty sparkly sandals.

"Do you have a coat or wrap?" Emerson asks.

"I forgot to pack one."

"I'll be right back." She disappears down the hallway.

Dillon has been in the living room and walks out. "I hope you know you didn't have to hide from us."

"I wasn't hiding. I had a few things to get done."

His expression says he knows I'm lying, but I can only apologize for the situation and thank them for their hospitality so much.

Emerson returns and hands me a stunning pink pashmina scarf. "This should look great on you and will keep you warm as we dash in and out of the restaurant."

"Thank you."

We pile into their SUV, and they talk about some work issues that came up after I left earlier this week. I watch the people walk by. They're tall, short, male, female, many nationalities, and no one pays attention to anyone else. That used to be my world. I already miss the anonymity I used to have.

We drive into the financial district down a one-way street and stop before a storefront. From the partially frosted windows I can see copper pots hanging, but the restaurant's hidden in plain sight. Dillon leaves the car with the valet, and we walk into the restaurant. The light is a subtle shade of gold, and the mixture of the exposed brick with the refined starched white tablecloth-covered tables and subtle contemporary floral arrangements is visually stunning and drips expensive.

"Miss Emerson," the maître d' says.

"Simon, so good to see you. It's been too long."

"Miss CeCe's here often, but we miss you."

She throws her thumb at Dillon as she teases, "Blame this guy."

"Follow me this way. Everyone else has arrived." He leads us through a small dining room to a nice-sized private room. I did a quick search on the internet, and their menu didn't have any prices, but the Yelp reviews say it runs $300 per person before liquor. I don't have a job, and I can't afford this place.

When we enter the dining room, everyone's already seated, and they've saved me a spot between CeCe and Greer at a large round table.

Greer stands and greets me with a big hug. "This is my fiancé, Andy."

"Nice to meet you."

Sara rises next. "Thank you for coming."

CeCe stands and reaches for my hand. Even though I've met her before, she's known in the press as Caroline, and I'm a little star struck that she and Sara's delicious husband are from *that* Arnault family. "I'm so glad you could make it."

Mason nods. "We miss you at the office, so we're glad you've come. This is my girlfriend, Annabelle."

She smiles broadly in greeting. "Hello."

We sit, and the waiter places my napkin on my lap. This is a much fancier restaurant than I'm used to. Everyone at the table looks at CeCe expectantly, who explains, "My mom recognized you when you came to the house a few weeks ago. As soon as she said something, I remembered you. You probably don't remember this, but many years ago, we met at an event that was being hosted by some technology group. You were maybe six, and all the kids were photographed together. It was titled 'Silicon Valley's Next Generation.'"

"I remember the picture, but nothing from that afternoon. I wondered how your mom recognized me."

"It wasn't that memorable of an event, really. But we're sorry you've been thrown into the deep end of the publicity pool. I promise it'll fade to an extent, but it may be a while."

"Do you have anyone handling your press?" Greer inquires.

I shake my head.

"Okay, I know the right person to manage this for you."

"Thank you, but honestly you all know I'm a receptionist masquerading as a project manager. I can't afford anything," I interject.

Emerson places her hands on my arm. "Constance, we'll figure this out, but for now, you need someone."

My heart races. I think I'm seeing double and may pass out.

Greer continues, "When you're approached by the press, you always ignore, give them your publicist's card, or say 'no comment.' If they ask about SHN, you can refer them to me."

"Don't hide," Trey stresses. "The press is voracious, so if you do hide, they'll hang out longer."

"That's true. Just go about your normal daily activities. Be out and about. When people stop you like I understand they did at Starbucks and lunch today, be gracious. Everyone has a phone with a camera these days. If it gets to be too much, call 911, and they'll push them back," CeCe adds.

"You still have your job at SHN. Coming back to work may be helpful to get away and keep you busy," Mason shares.

I'm too embarrassed to return to work. "I don't know if I can go back to SHN."

"Well, we can always go shopping and spend the day at the Burke Williams Spa," Annabelle offers.

The idea of shopping and getting a facial makes me cringe, and I catch Emerson pursing her lips. "I don't know what I'm going to do."

"You're going to stay with us in our guest room for a few days, aren't you?" Dillon asks.

"You can stay at my place. I'm heading back to Napa tomorrow, and you can stay by yourself," Greer offers.

"Thank you." I feel a little bit better knowing that for the first time, I don't need to handle this all on my own. "I've never been close to my father. He's not doing well and is getting his affairs in order. I've learned that he plans on leaving half of his estate to his wife, Lauren, and their three kids and the other half to me. I've asked him to not leave me anything, but I'm not sure he listened."

CeCe reaches for my hand, "Your life's going to change dramatically. Always remember who your friends are today. The real ones will be there regardless. I'm happy to refer you to legal counsel that specializes in these kinds of inheritances. They'll help you keep some of those who see this as an opportunity at bay."

"Thank you. I plan on setting up a trust for my mom and giving the rest away. I don't want any of my father's money."

"I knew there were a lot of reasons to like you," Trey announces.

A plate's placed in front of me, and I panic. I can't afford this meal. Emerson leans over and says softly, "Don't worry about the cost of dinner. It's all taken care of."

I look down at my lap and finger the napkin, trying to push back the tears. "Thank you."

Dinner's a whir, but I have fun despite the craziness in my life. If I could capture this moment in time and live in this bubble for a while, I'd be so happy.

chapter

EIGHTEEN

PARKER

I'M EXHAUSTED. I've been working eighteen-hour days trying to keep up, and I'm regularly distracted by what I did to Constance. I had no ill intent, and I didn't understand why it was such a big deal that she not meet with her dad. He's her dad, after all, and he's dying.

That was until I saw the two of them together. I realize now that he's a stranger to her. He was cold, and there was no warmth passing between the two of them. I heard her stories, but I also knew the public figure and was sure she was exaggerating her relationship. I'm such an ass. I wish she would let me apologize. My dad wasn't perfect, but I always knew he loved me and would be there if I needed him. That clearly wasn't the case for her.

I've had many sleepless nights. Nights where I lie in bed thinking about how I should've done it differently. Nights where I stand up to him and tell him off. Nights where I apologize to her, and we make love for hours after she forgives me.

I throw myself into my work to keep those thoughts at bay. I know there are more clues in the code. I'm sure of it.

My inner-office instant messaging appears.

Cameron: Parker, please come in here.

I pick up my moleskin notebook and a pencil, then walk into his office prepared for another verbal attack. I got in a lot of trouble for inviting Steve Trades up after Constance said she didn't want to see him. Nothing I didn't deserve.

I knock on the glass wall as I enter. Cameron doesn't look up at me as he continues studying his computer. When I sit, I'm in his peripheral vision, and he finally looks my way. "I've been going through your analysis. You're moving quickly."

"I'm spending a lot of time on it."

"I see that." He stops as if he's searching for his words. "I know you understand you fucked up with Constance."

"I do."

"Killing yourself to find the mole isn't going to redeem yourself. You're working too hard, and I'm concerned."

"I don't know what else to do, but I do know I'm close to something. I can feel it."

"Have you talked to her?"

"No, though I've tried. She hasn't returned any of my calls or messages. Through a friend I learned she blocked me, so I don't know what to do."

He looks at me and clasps his hands together. "Her life has been rather upside down with all that's going on. She needs people she can trust and depend on—"

"I'm one of those people, Cameron."

He holds up his hand to stop me. "A few of the partners met with her. Her father has essentially thrown her to the wolves with his announcement, and it's going to get worse for her before it gets better. We've talked her into coming back to work, but you're going to need to give her a lot of space. I don't want you rushing over to talk to her. Let her come to you."

I groan internally, though I'm absolutely thrilled that she's coming back to work. I can finally get the chance to see her again and maybe eventually talk to her. "I'll give her all the space she needs."

"That means leaving her alone, Parker," Cameron warns.

My heart sinks, and I'm holding my pencil so tight it starts to crack. I have to figure out a way to make it up to her. All I can tell Cameron is "I understand."

He nods at me to signify that part of our conversation's over. "I see in what you've sent me that there are a few issues and a possible back door? How are things going with the Pineapple Technologies code?"

“I found something remarkable in some different references.” I sit back and cross my legs, playing with my shoelace. “I can’t explain it, but there’s a lack of elegance in some of the code, similar to the other code where I found the statement. It’s in about two dozen lines, though I can’t quite figure it out.”

“Do you want any help?”

“Right now I think I have it. If I can’t get it figured out by the end of the week, I may change my mind.”

“Okay, keep me posted.”

As I return to my desk, the office is buzzing. I wonder what it could be about, until I see an e-mail about Constance.

TO: All SHN Staff
FROM: Emerson Healy
SUBJECT: Confidentiality

Please be advised that privacy and confidentiality are taken seriously here at SHN. That includes sharing of any private information about another employee.

If you’re contacted by the press for any reason related to SHN or an SHN current or past employee, please immediately refer them to Greer Ford. We do have some employees who are dealing with issues, both personally and professionally, and are of media interest. Please refrain from talking about it, even with your significant others or friends. An innocent comment can be used against our coworker at any time and affect all of us.

You may see a gaggle of reporters and/or paparazzi in the lobby. Please do not engage them or allow them entry into our offices. As a reminder, each of you signed a confidentiality statement when you were hired, and any comments made and sourced back to an SHN employee will be terminated immediately.

Thank you for your understanding in these delicate matters.

I would never say anything to the press. I hope I'll have the opportunity to meet with Constance to grovel for her forgiveness. I haven't known her for long, but I do know I want her in my life forever. Communicating that in a way that doesn't make me sound like a stalker or crazy will be my challenge.

I don't sleep well at night anymore, too worried about what's going on and what it means to possibly not have Constance in my life. I toss and turn, then finally get up and sit at my kitchen table to walk through the code again.

All of a sudden, I think I've found a string worth pulling on.

At the first word in a line of code that isn't elegant, I can tell there's something going on. It occurs to me that there are some odd notations of these random letters, "EM" and "AA." I continue to look until I see the name Adam. Then I see the name Eve.

I sit back in my chair and stare at it. I want to call Constance and celebrate with her. If it weren't for her help with all the Excel and the pivot tables, I never would've found it.

Looking up at the clock, I realize it's after ten; I haven't showered, gotten dressed, or called the office to tell them I'm running late. I send a quick instant message to Cameron. **I'm sorry. I had a breakthrough this morning and got involved in the code. I found something. I'm sorry I'm late. I'll be there within the hour.**

Cameron: Understandable. That happens to me, too. Take your time. Very interested to hear what you've found.

Quickly I shower and dress. I can't wait to see Constance today, and I want to look nice for her.

Flipping through some printouts of the code, I see the oddity again. "Ambrosia" is spelled down through several lines of code, just like the threat we saw earlier. Then I see another line similar below it that spells "mcintosh." Looking back, I realize these are the hackers—AA would be Adam Ambrosia and EM would be Eve McIntosh.

Holy fuck, the hackers have signed their name to the code.

chapter

NINETEEN

CONSTANCE

THE PHONE RINGING WAKES ME from a deep sleep, and I don't know where I am. It takes me a moment to realize I'm in Emerson and Dillon's guest room. When I glance at my phone, I don't recognize the number and I consider ignoring the call, but something tells me to answer.

"Hello?" I croak.

"Constance? This is Lauren Trades. Your stepmother?"

I sit up in bed, not sure how to respond.

"I'm sorry to call so early." I look at the clock—just after 3:00 a.m. "Can you please come here to the hospital? The doctor told us the end is near, and your father would like to see you."

"I don't know if that's a good idea."

"You have every right to be angry with him. He was certainly not the greatest father to you, but I'm hoping you'll come and see him before he passes."

"I'll think about it."

"Please don't think for a long time. We're nearing the end." She hangs up, and I look at the shadows on the ceiling until there's a soft knock at the door.

"Come in."

Emerson's standing there in dark plaid pajama pants and a long-sleeve T-shirt. "Bad news?"

"Sort of. It's the end, and my stepmother suggested I come before he dies."

"Would you like a ride?"

"Honestly, I'm not sure I want to go."

"I can understand that. He hurt you, many times. But maybe you telling him you're a survivor will help you in the long run."

I take a deep breath. "That's what Parker thinks. The person who actually wants to be there isn't invited."

"Your mom?"

I nod.

"Well, maybe you can carry a message for her?"

I pull the sheets back and slowly pick myself up out of bed.

I take a quick shower and throw my wet hair up in a messy bun, psyching myself up for this visit. Dillon and Emerson are up and drinking coffee. They prepared me a to-go cup.

"We'll drive you so you don't have to worry about parking. We can pick you up, or you can take a rideshare whenever you're ready to leave," Dillon tells me.

"Thank you."

Driving down to the hospital in Palo Alto is easy at four o'clock in the morning. The city streets are somewhat deserted, and once we leave the city and drive down the peninsula through the suburbs, I find the darkness strange. Living in the heart of a city, I've grown used to having the warming orange glow of streetlamps outside my window, their light filtering in through the gaps in the curtains. Here, there's a blackness that I rarely see, one that's almost absolute. When I tilt my head skyward, I can clearly see millions of bright stars dotted on the black canvas of night. We don't talk during the drive, and a soft rock music station plays over the radio.

We make it to the hospital in record time. They drop me at the main entrance, and I notice a little bit of a media circus. People are lining up to photograph something. Somehow the media has gotten wind that Steve Trades is in the hospital and it's the end of his life.

I spot the reception desk and ask for my father, and she points me outside.

"I'm his daughter, Constance Hathaway. I was called by his wife, Lauren Trades, to come down."

Again, the woman points me outside with the rest of the media.

If I came all this way and I'm not admitted, I'm going to be royally pissed.

It then dawns on me to call the number Lauren called me from.

"Hello?" she answers.

"Hi, it's Constance. The hospital's locked up pretty tight. Where do I find you? They won't tell me anything."

"I'm sorry. I didn't realize. Come up to the fifth floor. We're in room 523."

I ask the woman at reception where the elevators are located, and she must be considering if she needs to call security. I lean in and tell her that my stepmother said they're in room 523.

"I'm sorry. Yes, we have a VIP in that room. Follow the green line, and it'll take you to the correct elevators." She looks at me with sad eyes. "Good luck."

I nod and walk slowly, following the green line on the floor to the elevators. Given the early hour, I'm surprised as I look around the hospital. It's quiet yet active at the same time. There's a person mopping the floor, people wandering, doctors in their scrubs and white coats talking.

I find the elevator and take it to the fifth floor. I don't even need to guess which room is 523, recognizing one of the two members of his security team standing out front. Mark has been with my dad for as long as I can remember.

He nods and allows me to pass. The antiseptic smell of the hospital makes me sick to my stomach as I enter the room. A doctor and a nurse are standing next to his bed, surrounded by a few people I don't know.

Lauren sees me and stands. "Steve, look who's here. Connie has come to see you."

Every eye in the room turns to me and stares.

"My firstborn is here," Steve rasps just above a whisper. He holds his feeble hand out to me. I don't know what to do other than reach for it. He smiles and closes his eyes.

Lauren turns to me and says, "Thank you for coming. I don't think you've met your half-brother and sisters."

I shake my head.

She points to three kids who look a little bit like me. "This is Erin."

Erin nods. "Hi."

"This is Reed."

"Nice to meet you," he mutters.

"And this is Grace."

She looks up at me and gives me a half smile.

"And this beautiful woman here is Rebecca. She's your aunt."

I'm stunned by this, never knowing Steve had a sister.

Rebecca pulls me into a tight embrace. "We've got a lot to catch up on. I wish we were finally meeting under better circumstances."

I paint a plastic smile on my face, and before I can say anything, my father rustles in the bed and says something quietly to Lauren. She looks at me and winks. "Okay, let's give your father a few minutes with Connie."

I want to tell them they can stay, but they file out of the room and follow their mother, with Rebecca pulling up the rear.

Steve pats the bed next to him, his way of asking me to sit.

"I've always loved your mother. She was my muse and soul mate, the person who made me a better person, but we never did well together long-term. You were created out of our love for each other. I know I was a terrible father. I tried, but I had no examples of how to be a good father. That's not an excuse, but my reality. I hope that by leaving you half my estate, you will take care of your mother and one day can find it in your heart to forgive me."

"You were a shitty father, and I hate what you did to my mother over and over again. We don't need your money. We'll be fine."

"I know that, Connie. Take the money."

He closes his eyes, obviously done with the conversation. My dislike for him remains high. He loved the spotlight but I don't, and I worry about what that spotlight will do to my mother.

As I sit here, I don't know what to do. I will him to open his eyes and fight with me, but he won't. Lauren comes back with the kids. Their eyes are bloodshot from crying, and they hold each other and Steve's hands. I stand in the back corner, not sure what to do. Should I reach out to them and offer some sort of comfort? Should I leave and give them this time alone?

Lauren comes over and stands with me, holding my hand; I barely register that Rebecca's holding my other one. We watch as his breathing slows and he takes his last breath while holding Grace's, Reed's, and Erin's hands.

The alarm sounds on a machine, and a line goes flat. I hear a gasp from Lauren as tears streak down her cheeks. Rebecca's stoic but holds my hand so tightly that it would be uncomfortable under normal circumstances, but right now it comforts me. I have no feeling or remorse. Maybe I will later.

Turning to her, I tell her, "I'm sorry for your loss."

She gives me a sympathetic smile. "It's your loss, too."

I take a big breath and want to tell her how I have only a feeling of relief, not one of mourning, but I ultimately keep it to myself.

The doctor alerts us that we can stay as long as we want, but I'm ready to go home, or maybe back to work. I want to be anywhere but here.

I'm told that a media person's here who will make the announcement of his death on behalf of the hospital. The gaggle of reporters goes crazy when the woman starts speaking.

"Today at 10:43 a.m., Steve Trades passed away. He was with his wife of 21 years, Lauren Peters Trades, and their children, Grace, Reed, and Erin. Also with him were Steve's sister, Rebecca Simpson, and his eldest daughter, Constance Hathaway. At this time, the family requests—"

"What the fuck?" I mutter. *Who gave her my name? Who said she could share my name with the press?* I'm mortified and angry that they would include me knowing it would create a larger media storm for me. I don't want to be known worldwide as his illegitimate daughter, but that will be my new moniker from now on.

I want to leave, but the horde of people amassing in the parking lot is terrifying. I can't see any way out of the hospital without a police escort and a neon sign that screams "I'm Steve Trades's illegitimate daughter—come take my picture and follow me home."

As a last resort, I text Greer. **I'm stuck here. The press has surrounded the hospital. I'm not sure what to do.**

I'm comforted by the little dots rotating telling me she's typing.

Greer: Can you get out a different exit and grab a rideshare to Emerson's? The press is staked out at the office, too.

My stomach churns, and my head begins to hurt. They'll follow me no matter where I go.

Me: If they're staked out at the office and here at the hospital, I think I'm going to go hide at a friend's house here on the peninsula. It's only going to get worse.

Greer: Let us know where you are, and we'll get you your computer. You can work remotely and hide from everyone. Sara has opened up her beach house if you want to get away.

Me: I have a good place to lie low that nobody knows about. I can hide there.

Greer: Let us know how we can help. We're here for you.

My cell phone pings once more, and this time it's Tonya.

Tonya: I just saw the news. Are you okay?

Me: I'm okay. Not happy that they announced I was with him when he died. The press and all these people are here at the hospital. I guess they're camped out at the office and most likely the apartment. Do you think your parents would care if I shored up at their place until things calm down?

Tonya: Absolutely come! I'm leaving now, and I'll meet you there. Do you want me to pick anything up for you? Clothes from the apartment?

Me: No, work's going to send me my computer, and maybe I can have them add my overnight bag from Emerson's place. Do you think they could messenger them to your office and that way you can bring them to me?

Tonya: Sneaky idea—I like it! I should be home in a little bit.

I quickly send a message off to Emerson. **I'm stuck at the hospital, and I understand there's media at the office. Would it be OK if you messengered my laptop and overnight bag in your guest room to my friend Tonya? I thought, if you were okay with it, I could work from my BFF's parents' place in Palo Alto.**

Emerson: First, I'm sorry about your dad and all the chaos that comes with it. I think that sounds like a great idea. We'll upgrade security when you're ready to come back, so don't stay away long.

Me: Thank you.

I send her Tonya's office address and let her know I'm fine for a few days, so she doesn't feel like it needs to be done tonight.

In the twenty minutes since the announcement of my father's passing, the hospital is inundated not only by press and paparazzi but also by well-wishers and mourners of people who thought my father was somebody different than the man I knew. They're besieging the hospital with flowers, gifts, and cards for the family.

It's the first time I'm feeling overwhelmed. One of the nurses pulls me aside and offers me a ride to a strip mall where I can catch a rideshare far away from the eyes of the prying paparazzi. Rebecca overhears and shares, "I'll try to distract the press by walking out the front door so you can get out a back entrance."

"Are you sure?"

"Of course." There's sadness in her eyes when she looks at me. "Constance, I just learned about you tonight. I would've been there for you. I'm so sorry. My brother was an ass. I know there's nothing I can do or say to make it any better, but"—She slips a business card in my hand—"this has my personal information on it. I'm available to you any time, any day. I'm your aunt, and I hope that one day we'll have the chance to get to know one another."

I give her a big hug. "Thank you. This means a lot to me."

I tuck the card in my wallet, then follow the nurse to the staff changing room. She hands me a pair of scrubs and a sweater so I look like a nurse, then leads me to the staff parking lot. A few members of the press glance at us, but since I look like a nurse who's just getting off shift, they walk right by.

I get into her Toyota Rav4, and she drives me to a local strip mall.

"I'll drop you off at Starbucks. You can blend in easily there." When we pull up to the curb, she squeezes my hand and stresses, "I'm sorry for your loss. Good luck."

"Thank you for your kindness. I'll get you back the scrubs and sweater."

"Don't worry about it. I'm glad I could help."

I want to tell her the truth about my relationship with my father, but I'm not sure I can trust anybody ever again, so I just smile and wave as she drives off.

When I get in line and order a drink, I can hear people talking about my dad. Without a doubt, he was a marketing genius, and he was behind the smartphone revolution, but it's strange that people who never met him are crying for him in a Starbucks.

I call for a rideshare and head over to Tonya's house. When I arrive, her mother greets me with arms wide open. "I'm sorry about your sperm donor."

I laugh. I've called him that my whole life, and while Mrs. Wei plays the conservative Chinese wife, she's pretty tuned in. "Thank you, Mrs. Wei. I need to call my mom and talk to her to see how she's doing."

"Call from the landline from Mr. Wei's study. I think your mother would like to hear from you. She's probably taking this hard."

I sit in a black lacquered chair and take in my surroundings. There are pictures of Mr. Wei and many famous politicians in China and the US, stars of film, television, and music. He's also a technology pioneer, but he took care of his family. I spot a picture of Tonya and me as young girls in a silver frame on his desk, and it makes me smile. The Weis have always considered me a second child.

I call Jeannie's landline, though I'm not sure she'll answer a number that she doesn't recognize. I'm dreading this call. My stomach's churning, and I worry the coffee I drank earlier may come back for a second round when Jeannie answers the phone. "Hello?"

"Hey, Jeannie. It's me."

"Connie!" I hear her tell someone in the background, "It's Connie," and then she comes back to me. "How are you doing?

"I'm okay. I'm at the Weis'. Have you guys seen the news?"

"Of course we have. Your mom's doing okay." In a low voice, Jeannie whispers, "She's struggling."

"I figured she might be. I can come up to Mendocino in a couple of days."

"Don't be in any hurry. There's a small gathering outside the driveway, and I'm concerned that if you show up, you won't get any peace."

"Thanks for the heads-up. Can I talk to her?"

It takes a few moments before she comes to the phone. I can hear the tears in her voice. "You were with him when he died?" she moans.

"Yes, Mom. Lauren called. How are you doing?"

Sniffling, she whimpers, "I just loved him so much."

"Lauren invited me over to see him. When we talked, he told me that he's always loved you and that you were his muse."

My mother starts crying, and it just kills me.

We talk for a few minutes, and she reminisces about all the great things that he did for her while conveniently forgetting all of the shitty things he did to me. He'll always be perfect in her eyes. I'll never understand their relationship.

chapter

TWENTY

CONSTANCE

MY FATHER'S ESTATE ATTORNEY ASKS that we read the will before the services. His funeral's a huge production, so the services are being delayed until later this week so it can all be planned accordingly. The only people attending the reading of the will are those of us who were there when he died.

I'm ushered into a large conference room. When I arrive, Rebecca gives me a warm embrace. "I know it's only been a week, but how are you doing?"

"I'm doing fine. The press has been a little more aggressive than I'd like, but I think it's worse for them." I nod toward Lauren and my half-siblings.

"I agree. They've had a real three-ring circus." The media follows Lauren and the kids more than me, and I don't envy them. By hiding, I'm under the radar, just how I like it.

The media frenzy is everywhere, and people are all over the news talking about his death. He's being eulogized on television and in print. There are those who saw Steve as their mentor, their enemy, and those who never met him popping up in television interviews. It's surreal, mostly because the man they're describing isn't the one I knew.

An older gentleman comes in and introduces himself to us. "Greg Moran, nice to meet you all." He motions for us to take our seats. "I believe Mr. Trades has made all of you aware of his desires for his estate." He looks at Lauren, then at Rebecca, and finally me. "Okay, let's walk through this."

Piece by piece, he reads the will. Rebecca's given Steve's seat on the board of his company, along with five hundred A-shares, each worth over a million dollars. I don't look at Rebecca, but I can hear her sniffles. She was close to her brother in his later years.

Erin, Reed, and Grace are each given $500 million trusts that their mother controls until they're thirty years old. He included some rules around it being used for school and education purposes.

To Lauren, he leaves the house, one thousand A-shares of his company, and $2.6 billion in cash and assets, all totaling $5.1 billion.

I'm beginning to feel relieved, as it looks like he listened to what I asked and didn't leave me anything.

The lawyer looks up at me. "Miss Hathaway, your father mentioned you were uncomfortable with his plan, but he insisted to me that it remain the same. You will be given $5.8 billion in cash and assets. Your father left some instructions to you personally, and there are no rules on how you spend the money."

I'm staring outside at the tree branch that keeps blowing against the window, only vaguely hearing what he said to me. "Wait. What? I don't want his money." I look frantically at my half siblings. "I, uh… I…."

Lauren reaches across the table and grabs my hand. "Your father and I had long conversations about this when it became obvious that his diagnosis was terminal." She takes a big breath. "I've struggled for years about your mother and Steve's relationship. He would like some of the money to go to her to make sure she's taken care of. She meant a great deal to him. I'm sorry I was so selfish to not want her at the hospital in the end, but it's hard to admit to the world that I wasn't enough for him. Your father was a complicated man. You're not a dirty secret, but please understand that we chose to ask you to take care of your mother so that Erin, Reed, and Grace are sheltered from the media about your parents' relationship." We're all crying by this point. "He had many regrets. For so long, all his work was about amassing great wealth, and in the end, it couldn't keep cancer away. Not being a part of your life was a major regret for your father. The money will never replace him, but he wanted you to have it."

I look out at her. "But why didn't he just split it evenly between Erin, Reed, Grace, and me?"

"Because the money he's left me will one day go to them."

"Connie, we'll be fine," Erin tells me. "You don't need to worry about us."

Rebecca takes a tissue from the box on the table. "Constance, your wanting to be sure that your brother and sisters are taken care of only goes to show what kind of person your mother raised."

"Constance, when you're ready, we'll work out a trust for your mother and how you want to set this up," Greg assures me. "Not only to protect you but to ensure you have income for your children's children."

I nod, but I also know I have zero plans to do anything more than leave my mother a healthy trust. Upon her death, it'll go to some lucky nonprofit, and the rest will go to people who need it more than I do. I don't want his guilt money.

We walk out together. Grace holds my hand, and it's sweet. "Dad was right. You look like an angel," she whispers.

I bend down so I'm level with her. "Grace, I never knew Dad."

"He wasn't there much for us either, but I know he loved us all."

Wow. He never made time for anyone. What a lonely life he lived.

It takes less than twenty-four hours for the estate details to hit the news wires. My e-mail's inundated with people who I barely know looking to connect, invitations to events, dates by strangers, and meeting requests from people offering to help me manage my money. Greg calls to tell me that the receptionist in his office sold the information, and she was immediately terminated.

Now the circus begins.

Tonya: You're on the cover of three tabloids. "Billionaire Heiress" "Most Eligible Billionaire" "Sweet Constance's Legitimacy"

Me: I'm going to delete you from my contacts and block you if you don't stop.

Tonya: You're buying lunch next time.

Me: Fine. I'll never be able to go out in public again at this rate.

I sneak up to Mendocino to see my mom. Jeannie was correct; there's a large group of news and paparazzi. I meet Bert at the police station, and we decide that going in covertly will give me some cover, but also not cause too many problems for my aunt and mother.

I lie on the back seat of his police cruiser with a blanket over me so he can drive me to Jeannie's home. The house is pretty far out of sight and in a thick patch of trees, so it offers a bit of privacy at least. It seems crazy, but one less photo of me coming or going is a plus. He leaves after we make plans for him to come back and get me. He's incredibly kind, and I'm pretty sure has a crush on my aunt.

My mother's a weeping mess, and neither my aunt nor I seem to be able to console her. He was the love of her life, and she's devastated.

"Tell me all about the hospital," she begs.

I walk her through everything. "Did you know about Rebecca?"

"Yes, she and your father were separated from their parents when she was five and he was three. He found her shortly after you were born, but I never met her."

"She's very nice. I think when things calm down, we might be able to all get together."

"I'd like that."

"I'm still hiding at the Weis'," I inform her.

"That's nice." My mother goes into a full crying bout then, wailing, "Why? Why? Why?"

I hold her and sit with her for several hours. I want her to feel better, but I know this is going to get crazier before it calms down.

Burt returns close to five, and I leave the way I came in, lying in the back seat with a blanket thrown over me. Back at the station, I get into one of the Weis' cars and drive out of town, all under the press's nose.

When I drive back to San Francisco, I stop by my apartment and see a huge grouping of media pushed back by a police line. My neighbors must love me, especially since I haven't even been home in three weeks. Seeing the crowds causes great anxiety, knowing I can't live at the Weis' or stay with friends forever.

As I pull behind the gates at the Weis' home, there's a car in the driveway that I recognize. Climbing out of the car, I see Parker sitting on the front steps waiting for me. He stands as I walk up, so handsome with his hair tousled and his hands in the front pockets of his khakis, looking nervous.

"How did you know I was here?"

"I begged Thad to find out from Tonya. Please don't be upset with her. I was worried about you."

"Nothing to be worried about. He was just the sperm donor, you know."

"I'm sorry for your loss, and now I understand why you call him a sperm donor. I wanted to apologize, but I wanted to give you space at work." He runs his hands through his hair. "I'm sorry I put you in a difficult situation. It was never my intention. Honestly, I assumed he was just an absentee father. I had no idea how absentee he actually was. He caught me and begged to be let in, and I didn't realize until I saw the two of you together that I'd greatly misunderstood."

"Yeah, I think a lot of people believe he was a great father, particularly now that the news is out about his estate."

"I don't care about his estate. I hope you know that."

"Good, because I'll set up a trust for my mom and give the rest away. I had a long conversation with several of the partners of SHN who have been in similar situations. They were good at sharing with me that I have to remember who my friends were before this all started. We are friends, aren't we?" I watch him carefully as he answers.

A look of relief crosses his face, which tells me he isn't in this for my money. "I hope so. I want to be more than friends with you, but I'll take whatever you can give me."

"It's all I can give you right now. I have no guarantee what my future holds. If you're able to settle for friends right now, I could use a friend."

"I'll be here for you, forever and always." He starts fidgeting, and I think he wants to hug me, but I don't move to allow any personal touching.

"Thank you."

We walk inside, and Mrs. Wei greets us and offers us food. That's the way she deals with the stress, and I could use a little comfort food right about now.

Mr. Wei returns that evening, and along with Tonya, we all sit around the table and plot our plan for the funeral. My mom and

Jeannie will be here early. I don't want the press to know where I'm staying.

"Would you like to come and sit with me tomorrow?" I ask Parker, who's been quiet during the conversation.

"I'll do whatever you need."

Mason texts to ask if the partners can come support me at the funeral. I'm grateful to have so many people surrounding me, and it makes me feel stronger.

Lauren calls a few times, as does my father's assistant, Ruthie, trying to help set everything up and putting the names on the guest list since it's an invite-only affair—for the one thousand people who knew him best. Ruthie has set everything up so cars will pick up the Weis, my mom and Jeannie, Parker, and me at the Weis' home.

CeCe has made arrangements with a personal shopper at Nordstrom, and they deliver a beautiful black dress, a nice pair of heels, and a large pair of sunglasses. Tonya sets my hair in a conservative low bun and helps me with my makeup. "You're going to be on international television, so you need to look incredible."

Three cars arrive to take us to the funeral at a Unitarian church in Palo Alto. Parker arrives with me, and the light bulbs pop like we're on the red carpet. The event planner is there, and she directs my mom and friends to their seats. I'm asked to join Steve's immediate family in the back vestibule, where we'll remain until we walk in behind his casket.

Everyone stands as the services begin. Several men who considered themselves friends of my father's roll the casket down the aisle and we follow. I notice people are crying, and I'm not sure what to do.

The services are nice. The funeral includes people from all over his work life. It's a giant production, complete with world leaders and the CEO of almost every successful technology company. I secretly swoon over the future king of England and was surprised to learn a senior member of the Chinese government is in attendance. Thousands of people are inside the church, and estimates of almost a million people have gathered outside. Helicopters can be heard circling overhead.

I'm grateful that I'm able to be here today with my family, and I'm more grateful that Parker is with me holding my hand. The man who's taking my father's place at his company speaks first, and he shares some interesting stories and reads condolences that were sent from all over the country and the world, including the President of the United States.

Erin speaks about my father and shares some stories. Both Reed and Grace read some passages from the Bible, but neither Lauren nor I speak.

After the services, we're asked to stay in the vestibule to receive those who attended. For almost two hours, I hear story after story about all these great things my father did for people. It's like watching a bad rerun of a television show that's miserably long.

Before I join Parker in the ride back to the Weis', Lauren pulls me aside. "Thank you for coming. I know this was the last thing you wanted to do."

"I'm glad I came."

"I blame myself for the relationship your father had with you.

"What do you mean?"

"When we started dating, he told me about you and your mom, and his feelings toward her. He's always loved her, and I think I was jealous of that connection they had. Your father was very complicated, and I struggled knowing he loved someone else. I pushed hard for him to spend time with my kids at the exclusion of spending time with you."

"Lauren, that's very sweet of you to think of it that way, but you and I both know that if he wanted to do something, he did it. I know he and my mom had an odd and strange relationship. They were two people who couldn't live together but couldn't live without each other."

"I think that's the best description of your parents' relationship ever."

"May I introduce you to my mom? I think she's hurting as much as you are right now."

"I'd like that very much."

I bring her over to meet my mother, and the two of them cry together, consoling one another over the death of the love of their lives.

I'm standing with my two sisters and my brother, all huddled together. Grace asks, "Do you think they'll be friends?"

"I have no idea," I admit.

"He was a son of a bitch," Erin shares.

I smile big, knowing I'll love her from this moment on. "Yes, he was a son of a bitch and a narcissist. He was so self-centered, and he hurt everybody who loved him and adored those who didn't."

"I'm so tired of hearing what great things he did for everybody else when he was never there for any of us," Reed maintains.

"We have something in common, then. Let's just try to get through this today," Erin objects. "It's going to be hard these next couple of months."

I nod. "I agree that it's going to be hard, not because he's died and we're left with our grief, but he was never here to start with, at least not for me."

"He was never here for us either. It was always our mom. It wasn't until he got sick that he seemed to realize what he was going to miss out on," Grace confides.

"Thank you, guys, for being so kind to me."

My little sister Grace brings me into a tight embrace. "I've always wanted to meet you. I'm glad we finally did."

chapter

TWENTY-ONE

PARKER

AS I WAIT FOR THEM TO FINISH UP, I think about how today went and what it means to have Constance in my life. Coming to the funeral was easier said than done. The line to get through security was over an hour long; it didn't matter that Constance was immediate family.

We're seated in the second row of the church. Tonya and I flank Constance once she joins us after walking in with her siblings and stepmother, each holding one of her hands. Her mom, her aunt Jeannie, and the Weis are back a few rows.

The funeral itself runs about two hours, and I hold her hand the entire time. In the crowd, I see the partners from SHN, and a few people I recognize from the news, but most of them aren't here to support the family—they're here just for the spectacle. Sad when you think about it.

At one point during prayers, Lauren turns around in her pew and grabs Constance's hand. I hear her say, "Thank you for coming. I'm grateful you're here to share this with us."

At the end, the family is escorted out behind the casket. Slowly, each row files out behind them. After the service, someone puts Constance, her stepmother, and her siblings in a receiving line. It's ridiculous. This isn't a wedding, but I guess it makes a little sense, considering they aren't having any reception following. It would be a spectacle, to say the least.

As I watch the family receive the guests, I see person after person come up and talk about how Steve Trades affected their lives. Constance stands stoic, watching and taking it all in. People are naturally curious about her. She was his secret. Most knew she existed, but they think she had a better relationship with him than she did. She never lets on. I hear them tell her they remember meeting her at one event or another and ask to get together soon.

When the partners come through, they give Constance a giant hug, each telling her that she can return when she's ready.

She tells Emerson, "I'll be in tomorrow. There's no use in staying at home."

"We can't wait for you to return to work."

She just smiles graciously. "Thank you so much for coming. It meant a lot to me to know that I had some friends here to support me."

It makes me sad for Steve Trades. Nothing about today's colossal service was warm—it was a functional kind of event, very businesslike.

Sitting in the churchyard overlooking a cemetery from the early 1900s, I hold tightly to Constance's hand. She doesn't look like she's eaten in days. The circles under her eyes are dark and well pronounced despite the fact that I can tell she's put some makeup on.

"I want you to know that I'm really sorry I didn't understand what you were saying about your dad, and that I let him manipulate me. I promise if you ever trust me again, I will never take that for granted."

"Thank you. Your being here today means a lot to me."

We sit for a while, just holding hands and watching the breeze lift the leaves on the trees. I know that no matter what, I will do whatever it takes to get her to trust me and love me again.

"I was wondering…."

"Yes?" She smiles at me, and I think she's just the most beautiful thing in the world.

"How about we go ice-skating?"

"Are you sure? Last time it was rather deadly."

"Deadly? You were great."

"You obviously have a little bit of amnesia."

"Well let's do it anyway."

"Okay, fine. When do you want to go?"

"Soon. Let's get you settled first, and then let's find a place to go."

The Weis have Constance, her mom and aunt, the partners from SHN, and a couple of friends over for a celebration of Steve's life. Constance's mom cries most of the time, and Jeannie and Constance are there to try to keep her positive. I think we're all worried about her mental health at this point.

Dinner's a spectacular eight-course meal catered in. It's not Chinese, which has Tonya and Constance giggling.

"Usually my mother has a huge Chinese spread for events like these. I'm surprised she knew how to order non-Chinese food," Tonya shares.

"I bet the caterers took care of it for her," Constance replies.

Thad and Tonya escaped at one point, though they've since returned. I can't say for sure, but I think they got a little randy. Thad's pretty brave given there are several guards standing around the house who could take him out with a flick of their wrist.

"When do you think you'll return to work?" I ask Constance.

"I plan on coming in tomorrow."

"Really? That soon?"

"What's soon? I've been off for three weeks. I don't have anything to do tomorrow. The press is circling, but I'm ready to get back to work."

"Great. Lunch tomorrow? We can head out to the pizza place. Or go somewhere for whatever you want to do." I see the indecision in her eyes and try to quickly recover. "I'm sorry, I don't mean to push. Just tell me what you need from me."

She brightens immediately. "Thank you, I will. Unfortunately, I have a feeling I'm stuck having lunch in the office for the next couple weeks until things settle down a little bit."

"I suppose you're right. We'll figure something out. See you tomorrow, and don't forget that you promised to go ice-skating with me soon."

I start to move away, but she grabs my arm. "Parker, I know I didn't say this before, but I want to tell you how much I appreciate you being here for me today. It means the world to me."

"I love you, Constance." I know it may not be the best timing, but I want her to know how I feel. She's my world, and the time we were apart killed me. I want her to know that I'll be here by her side, always.

I can see the conflict in her eyes, and she doesn't say it back.

"I've wanted to tell you this for a very long time, but with everything you had going on, I didn't want to add to your already full plate. I'm sorry I waited, but I wanted you to know."

"I can't think about this right now."

I kiss her on the forehead and say goodbye. I don't want to put any further pressure on her. She has more than enough to contend with right now. "See you tomorrow."

Lying in bed, I look up at the ceiling and think about Constance. She's lost weight, and that always concerns me, but she's struggling. Anyone can see it. She isn't as put together as she usually is.

It kills me to see her like this. I want so much to protect her and tell her that her dad never needs to hurt her again. I want to whisk her away to some wonderful beach vacation and hold her tight and assure her that I love her and I will care for her always. I want her to know that I'm willing to brave the chaos for her. I would crawl on hands and knees for her to have me, but for now, all I want is for my words to resonate in her heart.

Please hear me.

Please listen to me.

Please believe me, Constance.

chapter

TWENTY-TWO

CONSTANCE

MOST PEOPLE AT WORK HAVE left me alone and not asked much about my dad. I'm sure they were warned ahead of time, but I'm feeling like I'm starting to blend in again nonetheless. It's allowed me to work hard and do my job without distraction, and that's exactly what I've done.

After months of planning, it's time for the company picnic. I can't believe it's here. Tina and her team have done an outstanding job and have thought of everything. We're expecting our employees and clients, along with their families or guests. This event has become the who's who of Silicon Valley and the place to be. It starts midday and runs through until 10 p.m., when we need to be off the beaches.

The party's set up at Baker Beach at the base of the Golden Gate Bridge. It's a public beach, but we have bracelets that each event attendee will wear that gives them access to food and entertainment. There's a huge stage set up in a reservable section, and Monkey Business is coming to play.

With a world-famous band as our evening entertainment, we know we'll see a lot of other people trying to come in, but Jim and his security team are prepared.

I see Parker with Thad and Tonya in tow. "How did you guys get in?"

"I'm one of the early employees of Accurate Software, and we were invited." He grins from ear-to-ear, knowing it's a big deal.

"Very nice!"

Pulling Tonya aside, I ask, "When are you telling your parents?"

"They met Thad last night. He and my dad geeked out, and my dad reluctantly likes him. He brought a fruit basket for my father, along with some Italian wine and an expensive tea my mother loves."

"Did you tell him what to buy?" I'm shocked he brought gifts for her parents. That's very important in Chinese culture.

"Not exactly. He did some research, but also remembered I told him my mother's favorite tea once."

I'm thoroughly impressed with Thad's initiative. "How did your parents take it all?"

"Surprisingly well. I also brought up the possibility of moving into the apartment, and my father nodded."

"He nodded? That's huge." I'm stunned. Not only are they not freaking out about Thad, but the idea that their daughter may be moving out is a big deal. It was always a verboten subject. My, have things changed. I'm so excited for Tonya. She's so happy, and she deserves someone like Thad who isn't intimidated by her father and treats her well.

"I know. It's incredibly huge," Tonya gushes.

"I'm so happy for you."

"Thank you. How are things going with Parker?" She leans in close so the guys don't overhear.

"Not bad. We're taking it slow, but he used the L-word."

Tonya's eyes are as big as saucers. "When? You didn't tell me." She waits a few minutes before realizing what I said. "Wait. You didn't say it back?"

"I have my dad's warning on repeat in my head that men will only love me for the money they think I have."

"That isn't true. Please don't start believing your dad's bullshit."

"But what if Parker does only love me because of the money my dad left me?"

"Why the self-doubt? What did Parker say?"

"Nothing really. It was very recent. He didn't want to overwhelm me with everything I have going on with my father, but he wanted me to know how he feels."

"You both were in a good place before your dad fucked it up. Don't you think his feelings could be genuine?"

"I want to think so. I mean, my gut says it is. I've been extremely clear that I'm setting up a trust for my mom and giving the rest away, and he's been really understanding and supportive of that decision." I have to believe that he felt this way about me before he ever knew about my dad. At some point, I have to trust that and let my father's paranoia not affect me.

She nods her approval before the guys whisk her off to enjoy the games and I got back to concentrating on my party.

The party goes well into the night. Monkey Business wraps up their last song right on time for noise ordinances, and security starts moving people off the beach. By ten thirty, only the fencing vendor is left wrapping things up.

I walk up to Emerson and Tina. "Such an outstanding job again this year," Emerson praises the planner.

"You know this is my favorite event I do each year," Tina enthusiastically replies.

"Let's make sure we get a date established for next year. Mason wants to do something really big, and we should get on people's calendars early," Emerson says.

"Sounds like a plan," I tell her, then look over at Tina. "Let me know when you would like to sit and go through everything."

"I should have everything wrapped up and final bills by Tuesday. I'll e-mail you to get on your calendar."

"Great." I turn to Emerson. "Do you need anything else? I don't know how Tina's still standing, but we've been here since six this morning, and I'm beat. The fence company is the last vendor, and they figure they have three hours of work. I'm fine to stick around if you think I should."

"No, go home. They have a fixed price, so if it takes them eight hours, that's their issue," Tina assures us.

Emerson gives me a big hug. "You did great today. This was a huge success. Thank you for all your hard work."

I blush from head to toe. "It was all Tina and her team. Honest."

"Well, get on home with that cute boy. We'll see you on Monday, or Tuesday if that's better."

"I'll be in on Monday morning." I wave goodbye as I walk away. "Thanks, Tina, for a fantastic event."

I'm so tired I can barely walk. Parker takes me by the hand as one of Jim's security team drives up in a golf cart. "How about a lift to the parking lot?"

"Thanks, that'd be perfect," Parker tells him.

We load up and the security guard shares, "This was a great event."

I nod. "It was. Now I want to sleep the rest of the weekend."

I hardly remember the remainder of the ride to Parker's car, or the drive back to my apartment. I drop my things next to the door and drag myself to the bathroom. "I need to take a shower and get the sand off me."

"Sounds good. Would you like a glass of wine or anything?"

"No, I think it would knock me out. How about a glass of water?"

"I'll bring it to you."

I don't close the bathroom door, too tired to care as I drop my clothes in a pool on the floor next to the shower. I start the water and wait for it to warm.

Parker brings my drink, and I down the entire glass. "Ahh. I didn't realize I was so thirsty."

Parker looks at me like he hasn't had water in a week and is dying. I can see a distinguished bulge in the front of his jeans. I don't know why I've doubted him. He's been such wonderful support to me and hasn't pushed. He's so handsome, and I want him.

I lean in and kiss him, my hand wandering to his cock.

"Do you need any help with your shower?" Parker asks as he pulls slightly on my nipple.

It feels so good. Biting my lower lip, I nod. "Please."

He quickly drops his jeans and T-shirt and follows me into the shower. I see his hard cock and tight stomach, and my core clenches. Even if I were to ever remain upset with him, my body would betray me.

Our lips crash together, and I allow his tongue entry into my mouth as I feel his hardness pushing against my stomach. I'm exhausted, but I need to feel the closeness.

Parker soaps up his hands with my shower gel and massages my sore muscles. He avoids my breasts and my sex, paying great attention to my calves, back, and arms.

"I need you," I breathe.

With his fingers, he parts my lower lips and finds my bud, circling slowly as he kisses my neck. I can't help but moan into him. He plays my body so well.

He puts a finger inside me and starts plunging in and out of me. "I'm going to come," I pant as he brings me up and over the edge.

My orgasm hits me like a freight train, and I want more. I crave more.

When I try to get down on my knees and return the favor, he stops me. "Let's move this into the bedroom."

I nod and we turn the shower off. I start by drying him off, paying close attention to his hard cock and balls. When I kneel to dry his legs, I slowly draw the head into my mouth and taste the salty precum.

Standing, he turns me around and leans me over the bathroom sink. He patiently dries my back and works his way down my center before plunging a finger inside me. "You're so wet."

I moan my appreciation. "Let's go into my room."

He leads me by the hand, closing the door behind us.

I may be exhausted, but I want this first.

chapter

TWENTY-THREE

PARKER

WE'VE BEEN TOGETHER NONSTOP since the company picnic. Lying in bed, her body's draped over mine and I'm stroking her arm.

I want her to know I'm there for her no matter what.

It's now or never.

"Constance, do you know when I fell in love with you?"

I feel her body tense, but I keep going. "The day you interviewed with Emerson. It was love at first sight. And I thought I lost you until you were there at the office. I was so stunned that I didn't even realize you were talking to me."

"You're talking nonsense."

"Don't say that."

"But it's true," she retorts.

"Okay. Enough of this." I grip her arms so she knows I'm ready to do whatever it takes to make her mine. "Your father was a Grade-A asshole. But you need to hear me when I tell you, I fell in love with you that day, and I fell in love with the woman who held me at night with all her might, afraid I might disappear long before her dad reared his ugly head. Was she a lie?"

"No," she replies sheepishly.

"And I fell in love with a woman who made me laugh and made me want to be better and do better. Was that a lie, Constance? Tell me, does that woman exist?"

"Yes, she exists," she replies, and it's the first time I see a small sparkle of light reach her beautiful eyes.

"Then don't tell me I only love you because your dad dumped a bunch of money in your lap. I don't want one penny of it. Don't tell me I don't love you, because all I do is love you, and I can't stop," I tell her, laying it out for her to see there's no going back for me.

I feel her resolve starting to break, and the last burst of its power makes her shake her head in denial. I take her hands in mine and kiss them softly, then place one of them on my eager cock so she can feel how it wants to worship her.

"I'm in love with a woman who knows everything about me, and yet doesn't believe me when I tell her I'm lost without her. Do you know how frustrating it is for the love of your life to reject you because her dad only taught her one thing, and that was to distrust anyone and everyone? No more hiding, Constance. I need your truth, and I need you to look me in the eye as you say it. Do you love me?" I ask. My panicked heart won't survive the damage this time around if she doesn't.

"Until my dying day," she replies strongly. "Yes, Parker, I love you with all my heart."

My blood rises, the ringing in my ears so intense that I think I've lost the ability to hear anything else but her sweet melodic words on repeat for a minute. But I can't celebrate yet. Not until we settle this once and for all.

"Are you mine?"

"Yes."

"But do you want me? I'm offering you all of me, Constance. Every imperfect piece of me. You already have my heart, body, and soul. They're yours regardless if you keep them or not. All I want to know is if I'm yours."

Her tears start to fall and a smile blossoms too, accompanied by her nod. "I want you so much, Parker. I love you so much," she cries, breaking the reserves of my faint control. Unable to stand being away from her any longer, I kiss her as if my life depends on it to survive.

And it does.

"What time are you due with the federal courthouse?" Cameron quietly inquires. We're excited at the prospect that a federal grand jury will hear what we've learned. Although we don't know who Adam and Eve actually are, this is huge.

"Walker Clifton asked me to arrive at noon, and I'm due in court after lunch."

"Do you feel ready?"

"As ready as I'll ever be. I have slides and copies of the code, and I've spent several hours working with the FBI and the US Attorney's Office. Hopefully this isn't too painful."

"Good luck. I'm hopeful that we get the indictment."

I don't get much work done as I wait for noon to come. I arrive early, and they put me in a conference room to wait. I can't sit down, so I pace the room, watching the people on the sidewalk outside and picking at the cuticle on my thumb. My heart is racing, my palms sweating. I've never presented to a grand jury.

Finally Walker Clifton walks into the conference room and shakes my hand. "Parker, I'm glad you made it."

"Thank you. Good to see you again."

"Are you nervous?"

"Of course. This is the big day."

"It shouldn't be too bad. Everything should go as we prepped. We have eighteen jurors, but we only need a majority to get our indictment under the Computer Fraud Abuse Act."

"But we don't know who Adam and Eve actually are. Will that keep them from coming back with the indictment?

"Not necessarily. It happens in these kinds of cases sometimes, since hackers use aliases. At this point, they'll be listed as unnamed conspirators until we identify them."

I wipe my hands on my pants. "Well, I'm ready whenever you are."

"Follow me."

We file into the grand jury room, and it doesn't look like anything I've seen on TV. The jurors are set up at a U-shaped table, a large comfortable chair in the middle. There's no judge present, just the jurors, Walker, and me.

Walker moves to the side, standing out of sight and giving the jury full view of me. "Mr. Carlyle, tell us about yourself."

I walk them through my education and background leading up to SHN. He then asks several questions on how I came to SHN, and how I came to be a part of the group working with the Cyber Action Team within FBI's Cybercrimes.

"My boss, Cameron Newhouse, asked me to review the code."

"As a software analyst, do you usually only look at software?"

"No, I can look at numbers too. I like to think that my job's to look at the business proposal and what they're trying to achieve, and if I think they can do what they're proposing."

"Wouldn't they provide you with a working prototype?"

"Some might, and others may provide a concept that may need more advanced math than they're able to make work. I then work with the finance partners to determine if it's affordable. My role in the company is to help evaluate whether or not my firm's interested in investing in proposed startups."

"So in other words, Mr. Carlyle, you're an expert at coding?"

"Yes, sir, that's correct. I'm an expert in multiple coding languages."

"When you went through some of the code for Pineapple Technologies, what did you discover?"

"We discovered a back door put there by the chief information officer. We also discovered two hackers who specifically targeted SHN."

"How did you know the CIO was behind the backdoor?"

"I found the back door when we considered their technology. He admitted it was there as a way to get into the software under difficult situations."

"Is that normal?"

"Artificial Intelligence makes people very nervous, and it's become common practice to put in a back door. But it's usually impossible to find unless you give a key to someone to find it."

"And you found the key the hackers used?"

"We did. And we found the e-mails he sent when he gave it to them."

"Very interesting." He looks at the jury, and they're all paying rapt attention. "You discovered two hackers, didn't you?"

"I did. An Adam Ambrosia and Eve McIntosh."

"How did you find them?"

"Through the TTP protocols. They signed the lines of code with AA or EM."

"You've lost me. What are TTP protocols?"

"I have an example." I show a slide with a bunch of code projected on the screen.

"Looks like gibberish if you ask me," Walker jokes.

"There were over two and a half million lines of code, and they're pretty complex in a binary language, so I understand why it looks like gibberish. But if you look at the TTP—which stands for tools, techniques, and procedures—you'll see their initials." With a red pointer, I circle the initial on the screen.

I look out at the jury and can tell they're listening closely.

I change to the next slide. "In these lines, you see a few acrostic."

"Can you explain what acrostic is to those of us who are less enlightened?"

"I had to Google it myself. It's when the first letter of every line spells out a word."

"What do the letters in this grouping say?"

I go through the threat message, and then I go through the names.

"Could this just be a coincidence?"

"I don't think so, sir. First, in their threat, it's spelled out plain as day. The names listed are SHN's founding members, and we invested in Pineapple Technologies. Second, in the acrostic of their names, it isn't very elegant. If you look here"—I change slides to another set of code—"you'll see how the commands are somewhat regular, but on the other slide they start with strange commands." I show another slide. "This is a list of common commands in the codes."

"You learned something else, didn't you?"

"I did. Adam and Eve call themselves siblings."

The jury breaks out in a murmur, and Walker smiles like a cat who caught the canary.

We got them.

The rest of the afternoon, I explain how I discovered everything, and I try very hard not to make it too complicated so the jurors are able to understand. When I finish my testimony, jurors are able to ask questions, and most are rather innocuous.

"Thank you. Mr. Carlyle, we appreciate your time."

I walk out after four hours of testimony, completely exhausted. Cameron's turn is tomorrow, and then hopefully we can get back to normal and Adam and Eve will be out of our lives for good.

Assistant US Attorney Walker Clifton and Agent Cora Perry invite Cameron and me over to the US Attorney's offices for an update. It's only been three days since I testified, and we aren't expecting much.

Walker says, "I have good news. Thanks to both of your testimonies, we received one-hundred-and-seventy-three counts of indictment against seventeen people. We know the ringleader is in Eastern Europe. He was responsible for trade secret fraud and sensitive corporate data breaches. Adam and Eve are considered fugitives and avoiding capture. Once they're arrested, we can either try them or, if we get close and the statutes of limitation deem it necessary, we'll try them in absentia."

"This is big." Cameron slaps his knees with his hands.

"Agreed, and you both were extremely instrumental. We couldn't have done it without you. If either of you wants to leave the dark side and come help us, we'd love to have you," Cora says.

"I think we'd be happy to help out on occasion with your Cyber Action Team, but for now, we're sticking with SHN," Cameron assures her.

"I had to ask." She grins and winks at me.

chapter

TWENTY-FOUR

CONSTANCE

I MADE A POT ROAST FOR DINNER. I'm not the greatest cook, but Parker seems to like it, and it's nice to do something other than order takeout. I look over at Parker, and he's cleaning his plate as if he hasn't eaten in weeks.

I feel really comfortable about where we are. I like calling him my boyfriend.

"Your dad's associate, Patrick, is amazing. I need to fly up to Seattle to meet with the Gates Foundation in a few weeks. Would you like to join me?" I ask Parker.

"You're meeting with Bill and Melinda?"

"Oh, I don't think so. But we can make a weekend of it and see your family—if you'd like to go with me."

"I'd love to. You can meet with the foundation, and we can go shopping for Christmas. Be prepared that my mom's going to want us to come back for Christmas."

"Well, do you think they'd mind if we brought my mom? We've always done Christmas together, and she's all by herself."

"Funny you should ask that. My parents were wondering when they might meet her."

I smile. "Then it sounds like a great idea."

***

"Are you ready?" Parker asks.

I pull a scarf around my neck and hope that with the ski mittens I found, I won't be quite so cold and wet this round of ice-skating.

"You look fantastic." He leans in and gives me a soft kiss, and I can taste the mint of his toothpaste. "Thad and Tonya are going to meet us there."

"Tonya has never skated, so at least we can support one another. She sent me a bunch of links from the internet on how to ice-skate."

He smiles broadly. "Did you watch any of them?"

I turn sheepish. "I did, but I think I learned more from you when we went last time."

"This is going to be fun, I promise. Thad's a good skater—he played hockey with me in school. He'll take care of Tonya, and I'll be there to keep you from falling."

I relax because I know he's right. Taking a big breath, I say, "Okay, let's go before I come up with a reason to back out."

We make our way downtown to the Embarcadero and the temporary ice rink. It's two weeks until Christmas, and this part of town can be crazy with shoppers filling the streets with their arms full of bags.

Grabbing me by the hand, he leads me out the door to a waiting rideshare. Our hands are next to each other, and I feel his little finger reach for mine. I know his movements, and I love that about him. He turns my insides to mush. I adore this man.

As we exit the car, I can smell the hot chocolate in the air. I have butterflies in my stomach. It wasn't bad last time we went skating, but I also didn't know anyone there. Here I can run into all sorts of people I know.

"Are you okay?" Parker asks.

I sigh loudly. "I'm fine. I just don't want to fall on my face and be humiliated."

"Why would you fall on your face? I'll make sure you don't do anything to be embarrassed about." He leans in close and whispers to me, "I love you so much."

His love and adoration make me feel secure enough to do this. "I love you, too."

There are people everywhere, and I see others hanging over the sides watching the skaters on the ice. We have reservations for the last session of the night. As I look out at the current group skating, there are several who are terrible. I stand up taller knowing I'm not the only beginner skater out here.

Parker checks us in, and we have just enough time to get my skates on before our session starts. As he helps me into them, I point out the little boy who can't be more than three years old. His ice skates have double blades. "Why don't they make skates like that for adults?"

"You don't need those. You've got this."

They clear the ice from the current session, and we patiently wait our turn. I hear Tonya telling Thad all about her internet videos, and we laugh. She's excited, while I'm filled with dread. I remind myself that I've done this before, so it can't be too bad.

Stepping onto the ice, Parker skates backward to hold both my hands for stability. We make it around the circle the first time, and then he lets go of one hand. "You're doing great."

I'm so focused that I don't see anything or anyone around me.

As the disco music surrounds us, I see Parker start doing his disco dancing impressions on the ice, and I realize I'm skating without his help. I'm much better this time than I was before.

He reaches for my hand, not to stabilize me but as a show of affection, and we skate around the rink. "You're doing fantastic."

Looking around, I see Tonya struggling, but Thad is holding on to her to keep her from falling. I'm glad the internet videos didn't help her either. "I'm actually having fun."

"Good! You're glowing." He takes his cell phone from his pocket and snaps a picture of me. Then he skates up next to me and we skate cheek-to-cheek while he takes a selfie of us.

"I'm going to post this on my PeopleMover page." I watch him write the caption "Before."

My toes are cold and getting numb, and I see there are five minutes left in the session.

Grabbing me by the hips, he skates us to the far edge, and it's like a fine dance as we sway to the music. My confidence on the skates continues to increase, but not enough to do more than really bob my head to the beat of the music.

The DJ announces that our session is up, and we're as far away from the entrance as you can get. People are filing out as the lights dim, and then a song begins—Bruno Mars's "Marry Me."

I'm shuffling along on my skates, trying so hard not to fall with the last few onlookers watching. Tonight has been so much fun. I was so nervous, but I'm really glad he made me come. Christmas is in two weeks, and I can't wait to spend my first Christmas morning with him, his family, and my mom. This will probably be the first one I'll enjoy.

Working our way to the exit, I notice Parker's skating around me and singing the song. He's goofing around, and he stumbles and falls. I'm nervous he might have hurt himself, and then I realize he's on a knee and holding out a ring to me. "... Constance, you're my everything. I want to spend the rest of my life with you, forever and always. Will you marry me?"

I didn't hear the beginning because I was distracted by what I realize was a fake fall. But he's holding a diamond ring, and I did hear the end.

His brown eyes shimmer and his smile makes my heart beat so much faster. I can't believe this. "Oh, Parker." I cover my mouth with one hand and look him in the eye. "I love you so much. Of course." I nod. "Yes. Yes, I'll marry you."

He stands and removes my mitten to place a stunning solitaire on my left hand. "This was my grandmother's, but if you don't like it, we can find something else."

"It's absolutely perfect." I lean in and give him a deep kiss, forgetting our surroundings. I'm so focused on him that I don't see Tonya, Thad, Tom, and Elizabeth on skates, approaching with champagne and flowers.

The DJ announces to all those in hearing range, "She said *yes*!"

I hear pops, whoops, and screams of joy, and I glance out to the crowd surrounding the rink. Behind the barrier are several of the SHN partners and our parents.

"How did you...?"

"Let's take another selfie." He pulls me in cheek to cheek, and I hold my hand up.

He posts to his PeopleMover page and tags me with the line "She said yes!" Laughing, I realize that's why he did the selfie earlier and tagged me.

I turn to him and smile. "My toes are numb, and I see the Zamboni ready to get on the ice. Let's get out of here and celebrate."

• • •

"As much as I want to go back to your apartment and celebrate naked, CeCe is having everyone over to her place. Is that okay?"

"I want to hear how you managed to do all of this without me knowing."

"I'm crafty that way. And Tonya helped a lot."

"I love it, and I love you."

chapter

TWENTY-FIVE

CONSTANCE

WE HAVE A SHOWING AT A house that I'm pretty sure is "the one," but when we arrive at my mom's, she's still in bed. She's been struggling since my dad passed, but I believe a change in scenery will make a huge difference.

"Mom, you need to get dressed."

"I'm fine. I can go dressed like this." She's in a nightgown without a bra, and the girls are pointing down.

"Mom, Parker's waiting for us. We're meeting the real estate agent at a house today in twenty minutes." I'm convinced this is what it's like to negotiate with a three-year-old.

"I'm worried you're going to overextend yourself with this house."

Here it is. I've told her that Dad left me money to take care of her. He was always so stingy; I'm sure she thinks he only left a few thousand dollars. "Mom, you do realize that Dad left me a very generous amount of money and he asked me specifically to share it with you."

"I'm not very good with money. He told me that all the time."

"I know, Mom. But this is going to be okay, I promise. Please get dressed."

Parker walks in and tries to divert his eyes. "Anne, I'm driving a big car for you—no sports car or Constance's Accord. And

I think you're going to really like this house. Let's get you dressed so we can check it out."

"Parker, Constance has no real reference for good relationships," my mother tells him.

I groan internally. When we got engaged last month, she pulled Parker aside and warned him all about me. What she doesn't realize is that she's actually describing herself.

"Mom, the Weis are a good reference," I argue. They've been married for over twenty-five years. They get along well and seem to still like each other.

She's doing pretty well, but we need to get a move on. She's still in her nightgown.

"I remember that beautiful flower-printed blouse that you wear with that flowing skirt. Maybe that would work?" Parker offers.

She smiles at him. "You know, that was Steve's favorite, too."

I pick up a bra that's thrown over a chair and her blouse. "I have it right here. Let's get you dressed."

"I'll leave you both to it." Parker steps out. Had he not come back, I'd still be arguing with her. I swear, I'm exhausted.

I hand her a denim peasant skirt, and she puts it on. "Where are your shoes, Mom?"

She sighs. "By the door."

"Parker, can you find my mom's sandals? She thinks they're by the front door."

"I got 'em."

"Okay, Mom, let's go," I announce.

Driving across town to the Inner Sunset neighborhood is relaxing. I'm not listening to Parker and my mother discuss my father. Parker's great at getting her to focus and move forward. She won't move into this house unless we talk her into it, and I think he's the only one who can do that. I'd be lost without him.

As we cross 19th Avenue, San Francisco becomes a little less urban, turning to quaint homes with small yards. The downside is that during the hottest summer months, the Avenues sit under dense fog the closer you get to the ocean. It's more than cool—it's cold and damp.

Parker and I looked at six houses in the area. This is priced a little high, but I think it'll do well for my mom. It's a Spanish-style three-bedroom home with a small front yard and a reasonable backyard with a fig tree and a small garden. She has a driveway with a garage, which is a big deal in a city with limited parking.

We pull up and climb out, and my mom stands back. "It's beautiful."

"Wait until you see the inside," I tell her.

We walk inside, and it's bright and white.

"Look here, Mom. This is a great place for your studio, and it gets so much light."

"It's just lovely. So bright."

She looks around and spots the sales sheet, and my heart stops. Shit. It's very expensive, but she doesn't need to worry.

She studies the sheet and looks up at me. "This house is way too expensive."

The real estate agent's quick to respond. "Anne, don't you worry. That's what they think it's worth. We'll negotiate that price down."

That seems to calm her. Parker takes her by the hand, and they walk through the house and talk about it. I hear him ask, "Would you rather live closer to your sister?"

"No, I think I'd rather live closer to Connie and you." They turn a corner, but I still hear "kids" and I cringe. If she's pushing him, I'll kill her. We'll get there in time. We want to be married a minute before we start having kids.

"Your lawyer mentioned you'd be paying cash for the house?" the agent asks.

"Yes."

"Were you lucky enough to work for one of those great start-ups that hit big?"

It's incredibly refreshing that she doesn't know who I am. "Yes, I was very lucky. I want my mom to have a nice place to live."

"What will you and your boyfriend do?" she presses.

We've decided, with my lawyer's urging, to keep a little bit for a nice house and a rainy day. We know we don't need it, but we can always set it up for our kids down the line, or give it away. "We haven't decided yet."

"Well I hope that, if you choose to remain in San Francisco and you're interested in a purchase, you'll consider talking to me first. I have great connections throughout the city."

I nod. “Thanks, I’ll do that.” I don’t commit to anything more. Now that I have Parker, I find it’s a real luxury to be able to make decisions together. That way if we decide we aren’t going to do something, I can always say he isn’t for it, leaving me less confrontational.

As my mom and Parker approach, the real estate agent disappears, giving us a chance to talk. “What do you think?”

“I like it, but it’s awfully big. I don’t own very much. I hate to waste all this space.”

“Mom, the trust will more than cover buying this house, and you can either go shopping on your own and pick things out, or we can hire an interior designer.”

She shakes her head. “I just don’t know.”

“Well I really like the house. I think I’m going to buy it, and you can live here rent-free,” I tell her.

“What if you lose your job and can’t afford the taxes?”

“Mom, my job doesn’t matter. The trust is set up to cover property tax, insurance, and all your bills. Dad specifically asked me to take care of you. That was his dying wish. I won’t let you down, I promise.”

She wraps her arms around herself and surveys the house. “It is rather lovely. The morning light that comes into this room would be perfect for painting,” she says reluctantly.

I give her a big hug. “I think you’re going to love it. And I can’t wait to hang out here with you and have tea while you paint.”

“Sounds like we have a plan, then,” Parker announces.

My mom pulls us both in for a hug. “You know, there’s enough room. You both could move in here with me.”

“You’re quite funny, Mom.” I look at Parker and plead with my eyes that he doesn’t agree.

I put a call in to the estate attorney and tell him we’re a go with the house. The real estate agent is outside studying her phone. “I’ve just called the estate attorney, and he’ll send you the paperwork. We’ll take it. I appreciate your help and guidance.”

The house will be bought by a trust that has an innocuous name. It won’t trace back to me and will be taken care of by the attorneys.

“Of course. I’m happy to help,” the agent says.

Through CeCe, I set up an interior designer to meet with my mom to get some furniture. I give the decorator some warnings about my mother's indecisiveness, but it doesn't even phase her.

The house is empty, and since we're paying cash, we went for a fifteen-day closing. When we take possession, Parker and I take my mom to a fun vegetarian spot she loves for lunch.

After we order, I hand her a set of keys. "Mom, the house will have all sorts of furniture when you move in." I can see the excitement in her eyes.

"I've never lived in a house we owned," she whispers, her eyes glistening.

Parker and I pull her in for a tight squeeze.

"It's the least Dad could do for us." I wipe tears from my mom's cheeks. "I've set up an account for you at Meiner's Art Supply. You can spend up to $5,000 a month there, but if you need more, just let me know and we'll figure it out. I also set up accounts for you at the grocery store. They'll even deliver if you don't want to mess with them. Tomorrow you'll have a small car in the driveway and a few credit cards."

"This is too much. I can't let you give me all of your inheritance. You need that to start your family."

"Mom, Dad left me with a lot of money, but I do plan on giving most of it away. Parker and I are working with the Gates Foundation for them to take the bulk of the money."

She grabs her heart. "Bill Gates was not a friend of your father's. He'd be very upset."

"I know, but Dad would've liked to mend that bridge, which is why I'm giving it to them. They're doing some great work. I talked to Dad's sister, Rebecca, and she'll get Dad's company to donate some hardware to rural communities in the world to help them."

"What will you and Parker live on?" she asks.

"We're doing okay, Mom. The estate attorney convinced me to keep some of it for our kids. I think we're going to buy a house ourselves and put some money away in case we need it, but we're going to be just fine," I assure her.

"I'd say so. Despite everything, you've grown to be an amazing woman. I love you so much, sweetheart."

"I love you, too, Mom."

• • •

VENTURE CAPITALIST

Book 6

Longing

(Coming June 2019)

A few words...

What did you think? With each book I write, I like it better than the last. As many of you know, when I outlined my series there were going to be eight books. I never planned on Parker and Constance until they were yelling at me to be told. (I have another with Jim Adelson that has been nagging me too which he will be featured in December 2019). This story is fiction and may have some similarity to a famous person but I truly made up this story and it has no basis in truth. This was supposed to be a short story but ended up at almost sixty-thousand words. I need to work on that—wink, wink.

It was really fun to explore secondary characters at SHN since my beloved team of billionaires can't do it all alone. While this story is more focused on the love story and only has the espionage as a side piece, I hope you enjoyed it. They make significant progress but for those of you who've not read any of the other books in the series, I hope you'll consider reading the rest.

I'm so grateful to so many people who help me with my books. In the last few months I've lost two very near and dear men in my life unexpectantly and prematurely. Without Michael and Steve's encouragement I'd never have written the series. They both died too young and I miss them terribly. But just so you know, they both died wanting to know who the mole is and never knew. (Not even my husband knows...) I dedicated this book to them.

I'd like to thank those of you who've read this book. I'm a little-known author in a big ocean on Amazon. Please, if you enjoyed the book, tell your friends. Help me get the word out. Leave a review. That helps wonders for people to find me on Amazon. I also love the e-mails and notes you send. I've rewritten novels from the feedback I've been sent.

I have a whole slew of people who help to get it out the door. A shout out to Hot Tree Editing. They take my written work and transform it to the magic you read (and hopefully we've caught all the typos). If you have a manuscript you are thinking about posting, reach out to the team at **edit@hottreepublishing.com**. I'd like to thank Becky who took the first go around on Flawless, she always gives me great advice. Kristin who does the heavy lifting with my line edit. She'd tell you I like too many comma's and some of those apostrophe's stump me. Also, no book is complete without the final eyes of Barbara, Rebecca and Sue. And Donna is the magic behind the curtain who moves my manuscript around and always works hard when I need to push the dates I've set for myself. Thank you, Hot Tree!

Many of you read the e-book, but there is a wonderful woman hidden in Spain who graciously does the beautiful interior of my paperbacks. Nadia takes art to a new level.

These beautiful covers are done by Resplendent Media. With Amazon continually changing their rules, Aria is grace under pressure, patient, amazingly talented and very easy to work with.

To my amazing friends who are some of my biggest fans, thank you Erin, Gayle, Elinor, Jean, Michelle, and the moms who secretly tell me they love my books. I love the encouragement and appreciate all the support and advice.

I have two beautiful little boys who play soccer, baseball, piano lessons, enjoy the occasional pottery classes, and always have some sort of activity that I'm shuttling them to. I grateful for the time they give me to write and share my creative juices.

I always want to make sure I don't forget the most important person in my life. My amazing husband, who leaves his shoes where I need to walk, or unloads the dishwasher while I'm trying to cook, fellow lover of chocolate and my guinea pig when I'm creating drink mixes for my books, without his encouragement and support there would be no Venture Capitalist series. He is my always and forever.

I'm truly grateful to you for reading my books. I've had these stories running around my head for years, and I'm so grateful for the platform to share it. Readers can be difficult to find, so I would be most grateful if you liked the book, you'd recommend it.

Ainsley

How to find Ainsley

Thanks for reading Venture Capitalist: Flawless. I do hope you enjoyed Constance and Parker's story and reading the five-point-five book in the Venture Capitalist series. I appreciate your help in spreading the word, including telling a friend. Before you go, it would mean so much to me if you would take a few minutes to write a review and capture how you feel about what you've read so others may find my work. Reviews help readers find books. Please leave a review on your favorite book site.

Don't miss out on New Releases, Exclusive Giveaways, and much more!

Join Ainsley's newsletter:
www.ainsleystclaire.com

Like Ainsley St Claire on Facebook:
https://www.facebook.com/ainsleystclaire/?notif_id=1513620809190446¬if_t=page_admin

Join Ainsley's reader group:
www.ainsleystclaire.com

Follow Ainsley St Claire on Twitter:
https://twitter.com/AinsleyStClaire

Follow Ainsley St Claire on Bookbub:
https://www.bookbub.com/authors/ainsley-st-claire

Visit Ainsley's website for her current booklist:
www.ainsleystclaire.com

I love to hear from you directly, too. Please feel free to e-mail me at **ainsley@ainsleystclaire.com** or check out my website **www.ainsleystclaire.com** for updates.

Also by Ainsley St Claire

***Forbidden Love* (Venture Capitalist Book 1)** Available on Amazon (Emerson and Dillon's story) He's an eligible billionaire. She's his alluring employee. Will they cross the line from boardroom to bedroom?

***Promise* (Venture Capitalist Book 2)** Available on Amazon (Sara and Trey's story) She's reclaiming her past. He's a billionaire dodging the spotlight. Can a romance of high achievers succeed in a world hungry for scandal?

***Desire* (Venture Capitalist Book 3)** Available on Amazon (Cameron and Hadlee's story) She used to be in the 1%. He's a self-made billionaire. Will one hot night fuel love's startup?

***Temptation* (Venture Capitalist Book 4)** Available on Amazon (Greer and Andy's story) She helps her clients become millionaires and billionaires. He transforms grapes into wine. Can they find more than love at the bottom of a glass?

***Obsession* (Venture Capitalist Book 5)** Available on Amazon (Cynthia and Todd's story) With hitmen hot on their heels, can Cynthia and Todd keep their love alive before the mob bankrupts their future?

***Flawless* (Venture Capitalist Book 6)** Available on Amazon (Constance and Parker's story) A receptionist with a secret. An analyst stretched thin. A billionaire's secret could tear them apart.

In a Perfect World Available on Amazon
Soulmates and true love. They believed in it once… back when they were twenty. As college students, Kat Moore and Pete Wilder meet and unknowingly change their lives forever. Despite living on opposite sides of the country, they develop a love for one another that never seems to work out. (Women's fiction)

Coming Soon

Longing **(Venture Capitalist Book 7)**
June 2019

Enchanted **(Venture Capitalist Book 8)**
September 2019

Gifted **(Venture Capitalist/Tech Billionaires Book)**
November 2019

Fascination **(Venture Capitalist Book 9)**
February 2020